BOBSLEDDING
WITH
THE *Billionaire*

ROSE M. COOPER

Book design by Oliviaprodesign

www.fiverr.com/oliviaprodesign

Published by Oshun Publications

www.oshunpublications.com

Other Billionaire Romances by Rose

Training the Billionaire
    One Night with the Billionaire
    The Billionaire's Bet
    The Billionaire and the Biker Chick
    The Billionaire's Billboard Proposal

Titles Available As Audiobook

rosemaecooper.com/audiobooks

JOIN MY NEWSLETTER
GET UPDATES,
FREEBIES & SPECIALS
rosemaecooper.com/newsletter

ONE

A Trip for One

TAMARA DECKER'S YEAR HAD NEARLY ENDED ON A POSITIVE note. For two years straight, she'd been on a winning streak and climbing up the ladder at the law firm where she worked. Everything was going great for her. She had a great job, a great apartment, and a five-year relationship with a handsome, successful man. Her life couldn't have been any better. But life has a funny way of turning on a person. In one big swoop, without warning, the rug was pulled from under her. Instead of ending the year on top, Tamara had three significant court case losses in a row.

The firm had nearly lost two of its major clients. One client's firm had almost closed down after a critical investigation. Her bosses weren't pleased with her, and she was lucky she hadn't been fired on the spot. Instead, her immediate boss suggested she take a leave of absence and put it on the firm's account. The firm was letting her take a plus one if she wanted to. Unfortunately, both her best friend, Nicole Parker and her boyfriend, Zach Craig, couldn't get time off work to join her.

"Thank you for taking me to the airport, Zach,"

ROSE M. COOPER

Tamara reached over to put her hand on Zach's thigh. She frowned at him when she felt him flinch. She removed her hand, asking, and "Is everything okay?"

Zach said nothing as he pulled up at the airport drop-off. Tamara's brows knitted tighter together, noticing he hadn't gone to the long-stay parking bays.

"Are you not walking me in?" Tamara's heart started to pound in her chest, and she felt a cold sense of dread filter through her.

"I know this is not a good time to do this," Zach wouldn't look her in the eye at first.

"A good time for what, Zach?" Alicia asked as the alarm bells were ringing through her brain.

"I need a break," Zach breathed, finally looking at her. "And I think this is as good a time as any to take it."

"I don't understand," Alicia looked at him, confused. *Was he saying he wanted to come with her?* "Do you mean you want to come on holiday with me?" She asked stupidly.

Tamara was trying hard not to listen to the little voice screaming in her head; *that's not the kind of break he means.* She'd thought something was wrong last night when he'd gone home early last night instead of staying over.

"I mean a break from us," Zach looked her in the eye. "I think it's better to start it now while you're away." He breathed. "I've got a lot on at work right now. I'm up for this new position, so I'm going to be too busy to have a relationship."

"You want to take a break from us?" Tamara looked at him, stunned. "How long have you wanted to take a break from us, Zach?" She hissed. Her shock and dread had spiraled into anger.

"Don't do this now, Tamara," Zach sighed and looked at his watch. "You're going to have to get going, and if I don't move soon, I'm going to get fined."

"Right!" Tamara hissed again. "We couldn't have you getting a fine." She shoved the car door open and got out, slamming it with force.

Tamara knew he hated his precious car doors slammed. It gave her pleasure thinking of him cringing. Zach got out of the car.

"Let me help you with your luggage," Zach said, rushing to help her haul her bags out of the trunk.

"I've got it," Tamara told him, pulling on the heavy bag.

"No, wait, let me," Zach nearly sent her flying as he heaved the bag and knocked her. "Oh, God, I'm sorry." He put the bag down on her foot. "Oh, shit." He fumbled and picked it up off her foot.

"I told you I had it," Tamara said through clenched teeth.

Tamara pulled up the handle, grabbed her onboard luggage, and started to walk away.

"Have a good trip, Tamara," Zach said as she walked away.

Tamara ignored him as she walked into the airport, trying her best to swallow down the lump that was burning the back of her throat. After Tamara had got her boarding pass and had checked in her luggage, she made her way to her airline gate. Tamara felt numb, but at least she'd managed to calm her anger. She was about to step through the metal detector when she was pushed aside by two big brutes in black suits and official-looking badges.

"Please step aside, miss," the man said, and Tamara felt like a little bug he'd just flicked off his shoulder as two more men in black suits ushered two other men through. The other two men were wearing oversized sunglasses, hats and were trying to hide their identities.

Tamara took a deep calming breath as the anger

started to burn inside her gut again. *Freakin celebrities!* She fumed. *Who the hell did they think they were? Get to the back of the line, buddy!* Tamara wanted to scream.

—•✦•✦•—

TAMARA LOOKED out the airplane window at the banks of fluffy clouds as they cruised towards their destination. She sighed. Tamara hadn't even been able to get her parents to come on the trip with her. They were off globe-trotting once again and enjoying their early retirement. Tamara was back to a table for one, movies on her own, and nights eating Chinese takeaway alone in front of some cheesy chick flick. She may also start investing in a few cats now because the dating scene in the modern world was brutal.

Tamara was about to take a sip of water when the plane hit a pocket of air turbulence spilling the water all over her.

"Great!" Tamara muttered and tried to stand up only to knock her tray and the rest of her water flying. "Oh, Jesus!" She hissed.

"It's alright, Miss," the flight attendant rushed to assist Tamara. "Why don't you go get cleaned up, and I'll take care of your seat."

"Thank you," Tamara sighed and pulled her carry-on bag from the overhead compartment.

While in the tiny airplane bathroom, Tamara discovered she hadn't packed any spare jeans or other pants. Instead, she only had the ones that were now wet in the most inappropriate place.

"Shit, shit, shit!" Tamara muttered, pulling out a dry shirt.

Tamara pulled off her jeans. She used some paper

towels to dry herself off before holding her jeans up to the hand dryer, hoping to get them dry. She hadn't realized the door wasn't closed adequately until it swung open. Her eyes grew huge with shock when they locked with the intense blue eyes of the tall, devilishly handsome man staring at her.

Tamara's skin popped out in gooseflesh. She could all but feel his eyes caress her skin. Shock paralyzed her for a few seconds while his eyes roamed her underwear-clad body. A noise behind him from the small galley kitchen snapped her out of it, and she grabbed her shirt.

"This restroom is occupied," Tamara hissed and slammed the door in his handsome face.

This time Tamara made sure the door was locked. Her heartbeat thudded in her throat, and her stomach felt like a thousand butterflies were fluttering in it. For a moment there, Tamara had thought she'd been having one of her flying fantasies. She always wanted to know what it was like to throw caution to the wind and have mind-bending sex with a sexy stranger in an airplane bathroom stall.

Tamara gave herself a mental shake and quickly finished getting changed. Her jeans were not a hundred percent dry. There was still a damp spot on them. But it would have to do. Tamara pulled her long jumper down over the wet patch on her jeans, grabbed her overnight bag, and left the toilet. Her heartbeat in her throat as she dashed to her seat, hoping she didn't run into the stranger that had seen her almost butt naked. Tamara had had enough bad luck for one month.

Tamara had breathed a sigh of relief when she got to the resort and hadn't spotted the man from the bathroom incident. When she checked in, she was pleasantly surprised to have been upgraded to one of the resort's super-luxury bungalows. These bungalows were usually only reserved for the resort's special guests. She found out later when she called her parents that it was with compliments from them that she'd been upgraded. But, of course, it helped to have a father who was a retired Los Angeles Chief Justice. Tamara did feel a little bad about not having told her parents about Zach or that she was in Mammoth Mountain on her own.

Tamara gave the bellhop a tip when he dropped off her luggage. She dumped it in her room and ran herself a bubble bath. She stripped off her clothes because the bungalow was all snug and warm. Even the tiled floor was heated, as was the toilet seat. She breathed in the pleasure of her surroundings before popping open the complimentary champagne and hopping into the bath.

"Ah," Tamara sighed, "This is life." She sipped on her champagne and let herself relax.

TWO

You Watch Where I'm Going

TAMARA WOKE EARLY THE FOLLOWING DAY DETERMINED TO find a ski shop to rent some skis and find out when the slopes would be open. After her shower, she changed into some warm clothes to go have breakfast in the main lodge. As Tamara opened the bungalow's front door, a blast of snow hit her in the face. She shivered and stared in dismay at the snow coming down. The snow was going to put a stop to the outdoor activities she had planned for the day.

Tamara pulled the collar of her jacket up and her wooly cap down as she made her way to the lodge. It was only a few short steps to the main entrance, but she was freezing when she got to it. Tamara decided she was going to swap her usual morning coffee for a hot cup of chocolate instead. She was on vacation, so she may as well spoil herself while she was here. Besides, after the last few months she had, she deserved to pamper herself.

Tamara pulled off her hat and took off her gloves when a man with a camera hanging around his neck and recorder in hand nearly bumped her over, rushing towards the front doors of the lodge.

"Hey, watch it!" Tamara moaned at the man. Bloody reporters! She thought.

"I'm sorry," the man turned to say before rushing through the doors.

Tamara stood, glaring after him and shaking her head. Before she turned towards the dining room, she noticed a sleek black limousine pull up. Her stomach grumbled, reminding her she hadn't eaten much since the airplane the day before. Tamara wasn't interested in who was in the limo. She wasn't a big celebrity follower and never understood how people could worship someone for doing their job. Tamara felt the same way about overpaid and revered athletes. She always felt that if anyone deserved to have fans and be worshipped, it was the people doing good in the world.

Tamara entered the dining room, and her senses were overwhelmed by the mouth-watering smell of fresh bacon, coffee, and scones. Her mouth started to water as she wandered through the dining room and found herself a table. She hadn't been seated for long when a waiter came over to take her breakfast order. The waiter told Tamara to help herself to the breakfast buffet and would be back with her hot chocolate momentarily.

After Tamara had helped herself to a generous breakfast of fresh fruit, yogurt, and some fresh scones, she sat staring out the window over the gorgeous snow-covered mountains. She'd taken a table by the big windows that looked out over them. The snow was coming down quite heavily and piling up on the windowsill. The waiter arrived with a steaming pot of hot chocolate. There were mini marshmallows in a bowl and a small bottle of whipped cream that came with the beverage. While Tamara enjoyed her peaceful breakfast, she heard a commotion from the reception area. She turned and watched staff rushing back and forth like ants hurrying to get food to their ant farm.

Tamara shook her head and sighed. Just her luck to have come to the resort at the same time as some spoiled pampered celebrity. Well, she wasn't going to let that ruin her stay. Tamara doubted any celebrity would dare to venture outside on a day like today. She needed to get to the equipment rental shop and wasn't going to let a mini-snow storm stand in her way. Once Tamara had finished her breakfast and got directions to the ski-shop, she headed out. The snow was still coming down heavily as Tamara pushed her way towards the shop.

The little bell over the door chimed when Tamara opened it. There were no other customers in the shop but her. The girl behind the counter greeted Tamara warmly and offered her some hot cocoa, which Tamara declined. She'd already overindulged in the delicious hot chocolate at the lodge.

"I want to inquire about ski lessons and booking some ski equipment," Tamara explained to the woman.

"I can help you with all of that," the young woman assured Tamara. "But the slopes won't be open for a few days, I'm afraid."

"I didn't think so," Tamara sighed, "not with the snow coming down as it is."

"It's going to be snowing for the next few days," the woman warned Tamara. "None of the ski lifts or instructors will work until the weather has cleared up."

"Can I book the lessons and equipment in the meantime?" Tamara asked the woman.

"Of course," the woman smiled. "Let's get you booked in and suited up."

Tamara spent the next twenty minutes sorting out her ski gear and buying some new outfits for the slopes. Her next stop was the antique shop down the road from the ski shop Tamara had been told to check out.

The black limo from the hotel flew past Tamara on her way to the store. Slush spewed up from the road and splashed her. Tamara swore a blue streak trying to catch her breath from her icy slush shower. She really disliked celebrities or rich people who had no respect for others. Tamara marched into the antique shop. Her body instantly started to relax from the warmth of the shop.

"Goodness, child," a kind, elderly lady said from behind the glass counter. "You look like you've been rained on."

"More like slushed on," Tamara rubbed her arms, warming herself up.

"Would you like a nice hot cup of tea?" the lady offered Tamara. "I've just put a pot on."

"Thank you," Tamara accepted gratefully. "I was told you might have some books?"

"I do," the lady smiled warmly at Tamara, pouring her a cup of tea. "I'll take you through to the reading area in the back."

Tamara followed the elderly lady towards the back of the store. It opened up into a small library with shelves stocked full of books.

"Make yourself comfortable and feel free to browse as long as you like," the lady told Tamara.

Tamara thanked the lady and set her tea down on the coffee table while pulling off her wet hat and gloves.

"Let me take those for you and dry them," the lady took all Tamara's wet clothing, including her scarf and jacket. "They should be dry in no time. You don't want to catch a chill."

"Thank you," Tamara smiled and took a quick sip of

the sweet tea. She felt the brew slide through her system and start to warm her insides.

"You have quite the collection." She told the woman.

"I had an old client who loved collecting rare books," the lady told Tamara. "When he passed away a couple of years ago, he left his entire collection to me."

"This is his collection?" Tamara's eyes widened when they fell on an old book.

"It is," the lady nodded before turning to go put Tamara's clothes in the dryer.

Tamara was surprised to find she'd spent most of the day browsing through the old books. The antique store owner, Val, was very knowledgeable on all her items in her store, including the collection of books. Tamara went to find her to buy one of her books when she found Val battling with her computer.

"You look like you're struggling." Tamara smiled.

"It's this new system my grandchildren insisted I get," Val muttered. "I'm supposed to update this new inventory system." She shook her head.

"Can I take a look?" Tamara asked Val.

"I would be eternally grateful if you're sure you don't mind," Val breathed.

"Not at all," Tamara smiled and stepped up to help Val. "I see." Tamara nodded after quickly scanning through the system. "There you go." She showed Val what to do.

"I'm never going to get this," Caro sighed resignedly.

"I don't have much going on, and I'm probably going to spend most of my holiday in your shop when I'm not on the slopes," Tamara grinned at Val. "I can help you get your system going."

"You'd do that?" Val asked Tamara with a look of

relief. "I don't want you stressing out when you're supposed to be on holiday."

"No stress at all. I love being in antique shops," Tamara admitted. "There's something about old things that fascinate and intrigue me. I always wonder what the story behind the object is."

Val had been both relieved and delighted to accept Tamara's help. Tamara was happy to feel she had made a friend and was not alone on her holiday after all.

The following two days flew by, and Tamara found herself enjoying helping out in the antique shop. It was two days before Tamara got to go skiing. She was proud of herself because she'd finally mastered the art of keeping her legs from sliding in opposite directions. Her instructor wanted her to try a steeper slope. Tamara was both exhilarated and petrified at the same time but was determined to try.

Tamara was doing great swishing down through the snow and keeping up with her instructor. Her heart was beating excitedly in her chest as she managed to take a steep turn without falling over or landing in a twisted heap. She heard her instructor shout something, but she couldn't hear him accurately. Tamara turned to look at him. He was gesturing with his head and waving his one arm furiously at her.

Tamara frowned at him until his words sunk in, watch out! She heard him cry again. Tamara turned to see what he was pointing at, but it was too late. Her eyes met with a pair of startled ones as she crashed into a solid wall of six-foot-two muscle. Tamara and the man went spinning off in an uncontrollable tumble through the snow. The man managed to twist in time to stop from landing on her. At the force he hit the snow, he would've crushed her.

Tamara was winded and laid in the snow for a few

seconds trying to catch her breath. Her ski instructor rushed over to her and helped her up before going to offer the man help. The man stood up and dusted himself off. Tamara was flexing out her sore arm when a shadow loomed over.

"What the hell was that?" a deep angry voice hissed. "This slope is not for amateurs."

"Excuse me…" Tamara stopped in mid-sentence, her cheeks flaming when her eyes met the angry eyes of the peeping tom from the bathroom incident on the plane. "YOU!" She choked.

"Have we met?" The man's cold eyes bore into Tamara's. "You look familiar."

"You're the man who barged into the bathroom on the airplane," Tamara gave him a dirty look. "Are you following me?"

"I'm sorry, lady, but I have no idea what you're talking about," the man retorted. "But I do know you should not be on this slope. You could've seriously injured someone or broken your neck." Then, he turned to the instructor. "You should've known better than to take a beginner on this slope."

"With all due respect, sir," the instructor's eyes narrowed on the arrogant man. "You were the one standing immobile at the end of a bend." But, he stuck up for Tamara, "This accident was more your fault than it was my student's."

"An experienced skier would've been able to avoid smacking into me," the man raised his eyebrows at the instructor. "You're both lucky I'm not injured because I would've sued."

"Sued?" Tamara found her voice after being shocked by the man's bad attitude and arrogance. "What were you planning on suing for?" She glared at him. "You were the one standing still on a dangerous bend that clearly states the dangers on the sign before and after the bend." She pointed the sign behind him. "It says right there to pull to the side in case of an emergency."

"Miss Decker is right," the instructor informed the man. "If anything, I should be writing you up for obstructing the course and not adhering to the warning sign."

"While I should be suing you," Tamara flexed her sore arm. "You damn well nearly broke my arm."

"Next time, watch where you're going. I suggest a LOT more lessons before you try the big people's slopes again," the man said hastily before pulling his goggles down and skiing off in a huff.

"You should be watching where I'm going!" Tamara yelled angrily.

Not only was the man rude and arrogant, but he'd also ultimately denied gawking at her in the bathroom on the airplane.

THREE

One Is a Lonely Number

RODERICK MILES COULDN'T BELIEVE THAT CLUMSY WOMAN that had plowed into him and then blamed him for the accident. As for that mouthy ski instructor, Roderick had in mind to have him fired. He was also a little surprised that the woman hadn't buckled under his icy glare as most people did. The resort needed to stop beginners trying out the more advanced slopes; it made them a nightmare for the more experienced skiers.

Roderick wasn't watching where he was going as he scrolled through his phone, climbing up the stairs to his cabin, and knocked into someone coming down the stairs. Roderick managed to keep his phone from hitting the step and nearly fell backward in the process. Instead, he gripped the handrail to steady himself.

"You again!" The same woman that had plowed into him on the slopes had nearly knocked him down the stairs.

"Are you trying to kill me?" Roderick growled.

"I tried to get out of your way," the woman scoffed. "If you didn't have your nose in your phone, you'd see that you stepped into me."

"What are you doing at my cabin?" Roderick's eyes narrowed. "Are you a crazy stalker fan?"

"Excuse me?" The woman stared at him in utter amazement. "I was about to ask you the same thing. Because this is my cabin."

"Oh no," Roderick gritted. "I explicitly told the resort I didn't want anyone staying in the cabin next to mine."

"Great," the woman glared at him. "So you're the one with the mountain full of luggage the hotel staff dragged into the cabin next to mine earlier today."

"I do not have a mountain full of luggage," Roderick eyed her distastefully. "Don't get too comfortable in your cabin."

"I'm already comfortable," Tamara raised her eyebrow. "If you're not happy with your neighbor, ask for a room change because I was here first." She pushed past him, nearly knocking him over again.

Roderick stared after her in amazement. The woman was a menace. Roderick also didn't believe in coincidences and wondered who she really was. He couldn't afford another detective snooping around him. Roderick's eyes narrowed watching the woman walk into the lodge. She didn't seem to be a detective, and he doubted any detective could afford to be staying in one of the luxury cabins. Could've been hired by someone who could afford a high-priced detective. Roderick would have to try and get to the bottom of who the woman was and what she was doing here. A plan started to formulate in Roderick's mind as he let himself into his cabin.

──◦◦⟩◦⟨◦──

TAMARA WAS STARVING. A morning of skiing had worked up an appetite that not even that arrogant jerk could ruin. Tamara couldn't believe the man had accused her of being a crazed fan. Who the hell was he, anyway? The lodge's front desk wouldn't tell her anything about any other guest, let alone the one staying next to her. When Tamara had mentioned to the front desk why she was asking after the man, the manager had assured her that she would not be moved from her cabin. Tamara's father was one of the lodge's most important guests, an honor that extended to his daughter.

Feeling a lot better because she didn't want to be moved from her luxury cabin, Tamara walked into the dining room to get a late lunch. She was also looking forward to having another pot of that delicious hot chocolate she'd become addicted to. Tamara was going to spend the afternoon at the antique shop with Val. Val made being at the resort on her own bearable. Tamara also got to go through all the unusual things and books in the shop. She ordered her lunch and some hot chocolate when she was seated at her favorite table by the window overlooking the mountains.

Tamara's phone rang as the waiter brought her hot chocolate. The caller was Nicole Parker. Nicole was Tamara's best friend and work colleague at the law firm.

"Hi," Tamara answered her phone while pouring some chocolate into the mug.

"Hi," Nicole's soft voice came through the earpiece. "How is your vacation going?"

"It's lonely," Tamara said honestly. "If it wasn't for Val at the antique store, I think I'd be going out of my mind with loneliness."

"I'm sorry I couldn't come with you," Nicole sighed. "You know how much I love skiing, but I'm a married woman now with a child, so I can't just pack up and go anymore."

"I understand," Tamara sipped her beverage. "How are things back in LA?"

"I've just walked out of a meeting," Nicole told Tamara. "The firm has taken quite a hit losing two of its major clients."

"Oh no, don't tell me we lost the Hickey account as well?" Tamara felt her heart drop to her feet.

"We did," Nicole said softly. "They decided another law firm would suit them better."

"Don't get all stressed out until we know what all the new reforms are going to be at the firm," Nicole advised Tamara. "I'll know more in the next few days, and I will let you know as soon as I have more information."

"Thank you," Tamara sighed. "I'll just sit on eggshells for the next few days."

"No," Nicole said sternly, "you'll go out and enjoy yourself on the slopes and putter around that antique store. You can also just relax, read a book, or start writing the one you always wanted to write."

"That's all great advice," Tamara said. "But I still need to know I have a job to go home to. I have a mortgage to pay, and I need to live."

"I'm sure it's going to be okay," Nicole said confidently. "Enjoy your break and clear work from your mind."

"That's easier said than done, all things considered," Tamara sighed. "But what choice do I have? We can't squeeze information out of the partners until they're ready to give it to us."

"Exactly," Nicole said. "Don't go looking for problems that may not be there."

Nicole said goodbye after Tamara and her chatted about Nicole's family and a few other non-work-related topics. By the time Tamara had ended the call, she was feeling so anxious that she'd lost her appetite.

TAMARA GOT ready to go to the antique shop when the snow came down heavy, and the wind picked up. The hotel advised its guests to stay indoors until the storm had passed. Tamara called Val to let her know she'd see her the next day. Tamara was secretly glad the storm had picked up. She wasn't in the mood for company and needed time to process what Nicole had told her about the law first where they both worked.

Back in her cabin, Tamara changed into a comfortable pair of sweatpants and a warm knitted sweater. She curled up on the sofa in front of the log fire the resort staff had made for her and opened the book she'd got from Val's shop. But she couldn't concentrate on it. Her mind kept slipping off to Los Angeles and what was happening there. More importantly, she was wondering why Zach hadn't tried to contact her these past few days. She knew they were on a break, but clearly, he would've still checked in with her.

Tamara was feeling low and lonely. This trip would've been a lot better if she'd had someone with her. Instead, Tamara felt like she'd been sent to a detention center where she had to spend three weeks in solitary confinement. Tamara was slowly going mad while her firm tortured her about the outcome of her future with them. Zach had added to the torture by telling her he needed space and dumping her right before she headed off. Tamara scrolled through her contacts on her phone until she came to Zach's name.

Tamara stared at the screen for a few minutes debating whether or not to call Zach. But her curiosity and loneliness won out. Tamara hit the call button and waited nervously for Zach to answer. His phone rang, and eventually, she was connected to voicemail.

"Hi, Zach," Tamara spoke to the answering machine. "I wanted to say hi." Then, feeling like an idiot, she hung up and deleted the message.

She was going to have to get used to being a table for one. Tears burned Tamara's eyes as the past few months caught up with her. She looked around the cabin and found a bottle of wine which she opened and pulled the box of chocolates from the complimentary gift basket. Tamara decided to spend the rest of the day in front of the fire. She had a bottle of wine, a box of chocolates and was going to watch chick flicks. She couldn't remember the last time she'd done this.

FOUR

Fire and Ice

RODERICK COULDN'T STOP THINKING ABOUT THE WOMAN next door. There was something about her, besides her gorgeous eyes and beautiful face. She held her ground with him, and it was as if she didn't know who he was. It was refreshing not to be recognized. Or the woman was an excellent actress. The front desk wouldn't tell him much about the woman, but they did manage to convince him that she was not a private detective or reporter. Instead, she was a guest and the daughter of one of their oldest customers.

Roderick wanted to know more about her, but she'd ignored his apology note and had refused his dinner invitation. He was sure she avoided him because she was gone before he got up and was sealed back up in her cabin by the time he got back to her. He didn't want to be seen to be harassing her, as that was the last thing he needed right now. Roderick was an Olympic gold medalist who built a billion-dollar empire from his skiing and snowboarding gear and equipment company called Spirit Gear.

Roderick wanted to compete again. But his skiing

future was hanging by a thread and the thud of a judge's gavel. A year ago, his life was on track. His star was shining bright. His company had exceeded his expectations, and his skiing career was everything he'd dreamed it to be. Roderick had been engaged to a supermodel until everything changed in a blink of an eye. Spirit Gear had managed to survive by him stepping down. He'd been close to being fired from his own company to save the business. Roderick's reputation was tarnished, and he was fighting sexual assault charges.

If Roderick lost his court case, he'd be ruined. Years of scraping his way to the top, blown by stupid choices, and trusting the wrong people. Roderick was no angel by any means. The past year had been challenging, but the previous year had been brutal. He'd been through hell. Then, while he was clawing his way out of it, he got kicked back down again. He'd started to train again, and that was why he was at this resort. A place he could escape and find his feet again while laying low and staying out of the media. Roderick couldn't believe how fickle people were.

One minute, he was the billionaire golden boy going places. Except for a few, his fans had shunned him while waiting to see if he was guilty or not. It didn't matter what his side of the story was. All that mattered was how the media spun a tale about the golden boy of the slopes. Roderick missed basking in the warmth of the limelight and his success. Now he felt like he'd been kicked out in the cold. Roderick was waiting for a jury to decide if he would ever bask in the warmth again. He couldn't even compete in any competitions until the court case was over. That alone was going to put him at a disadvantage. If he were cleared and could compete again, he'd be far behind his competition. On the other hand, he was sure he could still get enough points to get ahead of his closest rival if his court case was favorable.

Roderick downed a bottle of water and looked at his watch, wondering if the woman next door had got the gift he'd sent her with a bunch of flowers. He'd seen her walking into the dining room a few times and wished he could dine there. But he had to keep a low profile. Roderick stood up and walked to the front window in time to see the woman walking towards the lodge. She hadn't even acknowledged his gifts. Roderick was determined to get her to talk to him. She'd become a challenge and a mystery to be solved. He wasn't going to give up. He took another bottle of water from the fridge and sat down to order his dinner.

A knock at his door distracted him. He was hoping it was the woman that had come back, but instead, it was one of the hotel staff with a message from his fiery next-door neighbor.

Thank you for the gifts, but I cannot accept them. I accept your apology, though.

"The lady next door asked me to give you these," the man held up a bag that Roderick found had the gifts that he'd sent her.

"Thanks," Roderick gave the man a tip and closed the door.

Well, that didn't work! Roderick threw the bag onto the counter. He had to find out who she was. Roderick knew who to call to find out for him. He picked up his phone and started to dial. Roderick knew what he was about to do could come back and bit him. But he had to know who she was, and the resort wasn't helpful, so he had to go to plan B.

When Roderick hung up from his call, he felt confident that he'd get the information he needed soon. His phone beeped. Roderick had a meeting with his lawyer and then another with his board members. He had to put his brooding over the woman next door on hold. Roderick walked through to the bathroom and opened up the cabinet. He took out a bottle and took two of the pills. Roderick couldn't wait for the damn mess to be over. Maybe then he'd stop getting these damn headaches.

Roderick's phone rang as he made his way back to the lounge. He answered it.

"What news do you have for me, Carl?" Roderick asked his lawyer.

Roderick didn't like the man, but he'd already been through two lawyers. The other two Roderick had fired as they wanted him to plead guilty. *Why the hell would he do that?* Roderick would fight this and needed a lawyer who would stick it out and fight with him. He needed a lawyer on his side, not one telling him to plead guilty and settle. Roderick was not ready to watch everything he'd built through his blood, sweat, and tears crumble. Especially not because his lawyer, who was supposed to be on his side, quit when the going got a little rough.

"I hope you've been keeping a low profile?" Carl asked Roderick. "I managed to find that pesky reporter that found out you'd been at the resort. Unfortunately, he already had his story published. But we used your look-a-like to send him on a wild goose chase.

"Please tell me you didn't use Luke," Roderick swore. That was all he needed. He and Luke were not on the best of terms.

"We had to," Carl told Roderick. "Someone leaked your whereabouts. Luckily for you, your PR manager already had him on a plane to Mammoth Mountain."

"Great," Roderick's jaw clenched. "This is all I need for him to be here."

"Don't worry," Carl reassured Roderick. "Luke is not at the resort."

"I hope you have someone keeping a leash on him," Roderick hissed, "I swear, Carl, you know what's at stake for me."

"I have someone keeping a close eye on him," Carl told Roderick. "I've been trying to track down that witness you mentioned, but I've had no luck." He cleared his throat. "It's like they too have completely vanished. But don't worry; I have my best man on it."

"I hope so," Roderick breathed, "because we've gone from a whole room full of witnesses for me to none."

"Relax," Carl told him. "We'll find them. You take it easy, and as soon as I have more news, I will be in touch."

Roderick threw his phone onto the table and fell back on the sofa, cupping his face with his hands in despair. This was not good. There was still a bit of hope with the one last person that may be able to save him. Shit! He punched the air in frustration. He needed a better lawyer! Roderick was about to make another call when his phone rang. He frowned. Roderick was expecting a call from the board. He had no time for this call.

"I can't talk now," Roderick snapped into the phone.

"I hear you're looking for someone," the deep male voice on the other end drawled. "If you want to know where they are, call me back."

"Son of a bitch," Roderick snarled into the phone. "What do you want this time?"

"Why do you always think I want something?" the man laughed, "Maybe I only want to help you?"

I doubt that." Roderick's jaw clenched. "I have to go."

"Call me," the man's voice was laced with amusement before he hung up.

"Aggghhhh," Roderick squeezed his phone as if he was strangling the man who just called him.

Roderick didn't have the time, energy, or desire to deal with him right now. He was about to call Carl when his phone rang. It was the conference call he'd been waiting for with his company's board members.

Roderick answered the phone. He'd figure out how to deal with his other problem later.

FIVE

Bad News and Awkward Small Talk

TAMARA WAS TAKING HER SKIS BACK TO THE EQUIPMENT shop when her phone rang. It was Nicole. She was waiting for Tamara in the lobby at the lodge. A smile spread across Tamara's face as she raced back to the lodge. She hoped that Nicole was going to stay for Tamara's last few days at the resort. It would be nice to spend her last few days with her friend.

"Hi," Tamara rushed through the door of the lodge.

"Hi back," Nicole hugged Tamara. "I managed to get a few days off from work and home to spend your last two days of vacation with you."

"I'm so glad to hear that," Tamara was about to pick up Nicole's bag when one of the lodge staff came to help her.

"I'll take that for you, Miss Decker," the man smiled. "I take it your friend will be staying in your cabin?"

"Yes," Tamara nodded. "Thank you."

"Not a problem," the young man smiled.

"Why don't we go get something to eat, and you can try the amazing hot chocolate," Tamara linked her arm through Nicole's and walked her through to the dining room.

Tamara and Nicole were seated at Tamara's favorite table. They'd ordered a late lunch and hot chocolate.

"How are Elias and the youngest Parker?" Tamara smiled.

"They're fine. I felt as if my family was looking forward to a few days without me," Nicole took a sip of the hot chocolate, "Oh my God, this is amazing."

"I know," Tamara grinned. "I'm sure I've gained a couple of pounds from drinking it."

"You're looking lovely," Nicole told Tamara. "I was just thinking how relaxed you look."

"I feel a lot better," Tamara admitted. "I've loved skiing and helping Val in the antique shop." She put her cup down. "It gave me time to reflect on my life and these past two months."

"I'm glad you have," Nicole glanced at her hands and bit her lip. "I have to tell you something, and I don't want you to freak out."

"You know I'm going to freak out when you say that," Tamara rolled her eyes.

"The firm has decided to keep you on," Nicole swallowed.

"Why would I freak out about that news?" Tamara frowned.

"Because they are taking all your big clients away from you and moving to work in Paul's office," Nicole got the last words out as quickly as she.

"What?" Tamara breathed angrily. She could feel her cheeks flaring with heat.

"I'm sorry, Tamara," Nicole told her.

"It's because they want me to resign, isn't it?" Tamara shook her. "Those bastards."

"Tamara, you know you could've won those cases," Nicole raised her eyebrows. "You dropped the ball because you know deep down you sided with the defense."

"That's not true," Tamara said indignantly. "I would never let my opinions affect my case."

"I saw the look on your face when you saw that document," Nicole told Tamara. "I've known you nearly all my life. So I know when you're up to something."

"I didn't do anything wrong, and I was on my client's side," Tamara said.

She was a little hurt that Nicole would accuse her of the same thing her boss had. Her boss had also believed Tamara had deliberately dropped the ball on the three cases she'd lost. She may not have agreed with her clients, and deep down, Tamara knew she was glad the other side won. Tamara hated how big corporations got away with poisoning the world just because they could afford to hire people to make the world turn a blind eye.

"I'm sorry," Nicole sighed. "I wasn't accusing you of divulging secrets to the other side. But we both know you would have slaughtered the other side if you were all in. You go for the jugular every time, right at the last minute." She raised her eyebrows. "It wasn't like that with those cases."

"There was no jugular to go for," Tamara said. "The defendant had us over a barrel with nowhere to go."

"Okay," Nicole held her hands up in surrender. "Let's change the subject and leave work for when we're back in LA."

"Agreed," Tamara gave Nicole a tight smile. "I have something to admit to you too."

"Uh-oh," Nicole's brows furrowed.

"Zach and I are on a break," Tamara swallowed.

"What?" Nicole looked at Tamara in shock. "Who needed the break?"

"Zach," Tamara took another sip of her chocolate. "He decided that we should take this time apart to be apart relationship-wise."

"Oh no," Nicole put her hand on Tamara's. "I'm sorry. That was pretty horrid of him. To wait to tell you as you're about to go on vacation."

"I guess," Tamara sighed. "Five years I invested in that relationship." She shook her head. "Now I'm going to be the sad friend who ticks the box 'no plus one.'"

"Oh, come on," Nicole smiled encouragingly at Tamara. "You're beautiful, and Zach's an idiot. So you won't be single for long."

"Thanks for the encouragement," Tamara smiled. "But I'm going to concentrate on myself for a while." She poured some more hot chocolate. "I need to find a new job, and besides, Christmas and New Year aren't the time to be looking for a new relationship."

"I agree," Nicole pulled a face. "It's so awkward meeting someone during December because it's the whole gift and Christmas day thing!"

"I know, it's awkward," Tamara shook her head. "I think after lunch, we should head over to the cabin and get you something warm to wear before going to the slopes."

"I like that idea," Nicole agreed.

Tamara and Nicole finished off their lunch before heading to the cabin. When they walked up the stairs towards the cabin, Tamara noticed the man next door watching them from his cabin. Tamara had decided not to tell Nicole about the man who'd simply signed his gifts RM. She gave him a sideways glance letting him know she knew he was watching them doing his Peeping-Tom thing again. Tamara shuddered, hoping he wasn't some weirdo stalker. She gave herself a mental shake as she let herself and Nicole into the cabin.

"Wow," Nicole looked around the spacious cabin. "This is fabulous." She looked at Tamara. "Can we live here?"

"I know, right?" Tamara grinned. She'd had the same reactions as her friend upon walking into the cabin the first time. "Let me show you around."

"I'm going to move in here," Nicole breathed when they walked into her bedroom.

"Wait until you see the bathroom," Tamara told Nicole. "Each room in the cabin has a spa bath, and there is nothing better than a hot spa bubble bath after skiing."

"I can only imagine and cannot wait," Nicole sighed.

"We won't be able to go to the slopes, but we can go for a walk around the resort," Tamara suggested.

"I'd love that," Nicole smiled at Tamara. "Let me get something warmer to wear."

"I'll meet you downstairs when you're ready," Tamara told Nicole and left the room.

⸺•❦•❦•⸺

THE LAST TWO days of Tamara's vacation flew by with Nicole there. Tamara's bags were packed and ready for the resort staff to come to fetch the bags. Nicole had gone on to the lodge dining room to reserve a table for breakfast before they left. Tamara was walking out of the cabin at the same time as RM was walking out of his cabin.

Well, this was awkward! Tamara thought, plastering a smile on her face.

"Hi," RM smiled at Tamara. "I see you're leaving."

"Hi," Tamara said politely. "I am. Vacation time is over, and it's time to head home."

"Where is home?" he asked Tamara.

"Los Angeles," Tamara said, then wondered why she'd told him the truth. "Are you here for much longer?"

"Another few weeks probably," RM said, walking down the stairs with her.

"Well, I hope you enjoy the rest of your stay," Tamara gave him a tight smile.

"Thank you," RM nodded. "Have a safe journey home."

They stood looking at each other awkwardly for a few seconds before Tamara smiled politely and stepped around him to walk towards the lodge. Her legs felt a little shaky when she remembered the feel of his solid muscled chest. Skiing into the man had been like hitting a firm wall of muscle.

Tamara gave herself a mental shake again. The man's gaze when he'd looked her over in the airplane bathroom still gave her goose bumps. However, he did seem a little less uptight on the plane than he did when she ran into the slopes. He also didn't recognize her from the bathroom. It was probably because he didn't spend much time staring at her face, Tamara reasoned. Besides, it didn't matter. She wasn't ever going to see the man again.

SIX

A New Year and New Beginnings

TAMARA STARED OUT THE WINDOW OF HER APARTMENT. She'd been back from her vacation for a little over five weeks and tomorrow was Christmas. But, unfortunately, it was going to be a lonely Christmas for Tamara this year. She'd not heard from Zach since Tamara had gone on vacation, and Tamara's parents had canceled their Christmas plans with her to go on a cruise to the Bahamas. Instead, her parents would visit her in June the following year.

Tamara didn't want her parents feeling guilty about her being alone for Christmas, so she'd opted not to tell them about her and Zach's broken relationship. However, they did know that she'd left her job at her old law firm and was looking for a new one. Tamara's parents were always supportive of her and only wanted what was best for her. Her father had offered to make some calls for Tamara, but she wanted to get a job on her own merits. She didn't want to get a job because of who her father was.

Tamara sighed and turned back to her computer. She was sending her resume to two more law firms before she went to visit Nicole and Elias. Tamara was spending Christmas even with them. Tomorrow she will sleep in late; Skype with her parents, and have leftovers from Nicole's dinner for lunch. Tamara pressed send on her final application and closed her laptop. She needed to get ready for her evening with the Parkers. Tamara had been spending a lot of time with Nicole and her family since she'd got back for her vacation.

The Parkers had been very supportive of her, which Tamara was so grateful for. Without them, she'd have been a lot lonelier and a little lost. Nicole had helped Tamara a lot with getting her resume up to date and sending out her resume. Unfortunately, out of all the applications Tamara had sent out over the past weeks, she'd gotten no replies in return. She was starting to feel a little disheartened. Nicole thought that the law firms were closing down for Christmas and would put their hiring on hold until the New Year. Tamara hoped that was the case as she battled to keep her hope alive.

—•☾☯•☾☯•—

"I'M SO FULL," Tamara helped Nicole clear away the table and pack the dishwasher. "Thank you for having me over on Christmas Eve."

"Of course," Nicole smiled at Tamara. "We love having you here."

"I applied to the last two law firms on the long list you gave me," Tamara refilled their wine glasses. "I must admit that it's been hard trying to keep my spirits up."

"It'll come right," Nicole assured Tamara. "This is a terrible time of year to be searching for a job. People go away for the holidays, and law firm owners have probably headed south for the winter for the sun or to a ski resort."

She took a sip of her wine. "Unfortunately, that means that the people who need to see your resume have probably put all business on hold."

"I'm hoping you're right," Tamara smiled.

"Speaking of work," Elias, Nicole's husband, walked into the kitchen. "I know a law firm that is looking for someone with your skills."

"Really?" Tamara and Nicole said at the same time.

"Yes," Elias nodded. "They mainly handle high profile cases."

"That's better than destructive corporations," Nicole raised her eyebrows and looked at Tamara.

"It sounds interesting," Tamara gave a fake smile. She didn't like celebrities, but a job was a job, and lawyers who worked with high-profile cases brought in a lot of money. "Give me the details, and I will send it off tomorrow… or on the twenty-sixth."

"I think the twenty-sixth would be better," Nicole grinned. "They may think you were desperate if you sent it on Christmas day."

"I am desperate," Tamara admitted and took a sip of her wine.

"Yes, but the company doesn't need to know that," Nicole said.

"I've messaged the information to you," Elias told Tamara.

"I know this firm," Tamara's brows drew together. "Thank you, Elias."

"We'll send good thoughts your way," Nicole smiled.

—••◦◯◯•◯◯◦••—

IT WAS LATE when Tamara got home to her apartment with a few bowls of leftovers from Nicole's dinner. That was going to be her Christmas lunch. Tamara had a shower and put on her pajamas. She was eager to find out more about the law firm and the job Elias had sent her. *It looked promising,* Tamara thought as she started on an introductory letter to the contact name Elias had given her.

RODERICK WALKED around the stately mansion. He liked the flow of the house and the neighborhood. Roderick had always wanted to buy a home in Los Angeles but had never committed to it until now. His apartment had become a bit stifling, and most of the LA media knew where he lived. So Roderick was buying this property discreetly. He hoped to have at least a couple of months of anonymity before the press found out where he'd moved. Also, this house didn't have any close nosey neighbors trying to get the media attention off of themselves by pointing out another celebrity in the vicinity.

Roderick couldn't wait for the court case to be over so he could move on with his life and start fresh. He even had plans to create a new company, one that he couldn't get fired from. Roderick had been working on his new company for some time already. Especially when his current one took off and became the giant it currently was. His products had become an exclusive brand name which came with a high price tag. It was not what Roderick had ever intended it to be. He'd wanted a good quality product that everyone could afford. But with fame came the ego. Soon, his company was soaring to a billion-dollar corporation, and Roderick had gotten drunk on the lifestyle that went with it.

If Roderick was going to start again, it was going to be doing what he'd first set out to do. But for now, he'd have to put those dreams on hold until he knew what his fate was going to be once his court case was over. Roderick had asked the law firm representing him to find him another lawyer. He was not happy with Carl, and the man was leaning towards Roderick pleading guilty. But, there was not a chance in hell of that happening. He had at least another two years competing. He had plans that being convicted or admitting to sexual assault would end. Roderick sighed. In the New Year, he would have to start all over again with a new lawyer. He looked at his watch. It had been one of the loneliest Christmas's that Roderick could remember having.

When Roderick was the golden boy flying high, he'd have endless Christmas and New Year's Day invitations. This year, he had none. None of his so-called friends wanted to be associated with someone accused of sexual assault. Roderick would remember this. It had been a harsh lesson to learn, and he shouldn't have been surprised by it. Roderick had watched a lot of high-profile people becoming social outcasts when they'd been accused of something. He sighed and looked around his new home. It was so cold and hollow. Roderick walked through to the fully equipped gym to get some training in before swimming.

His contact had managed to track down the woman who'd been his neighbor at the ski resort. Now Roderick just had to figure out how to approach her without being accused of being some kind of weird stalker. Her name was Tamara Decker, and she was an attorney at some big-shot law firm that protected large corporations. Roderick wondered if she wasn't the kind of lawyer he needed. Cutthroat enough to defend companies against the atrocities they caused anyone unlucky enough to get in their way. As Roderick started training, he made a mental note to see if the firm representing him couldn't coax Miss Decker to join them. Well, that was if she was any good. Roderick was waiting for more information about Tamara Decker from his contact.

That would be one way to get to spend more time with her. A plan started to formulate in Roderick's mind as he began to work out. A smile split his face during his warm-up, thinking about the fiery Tamara Decker.

TAMARA SENT her resume to the company Elias had suggested the day after Christmas. She was surprised to get a response the next day. The firm wanted to see her the first week in January. The New Year's Eve party turned into a job interview celebration party with the Parkers at a friend of theirs. Tamara had even let herself be chatted up by one of their single male friends, so she had someone to kiss at midnight.

In the early hours of the New Year, Tamara let herself into her apartment after an enjoyable night out full of confidence. Finally, she was ready to get back to work. Tamara was going to get this job!

SEVEN

A Chance to Get Back on Top

TAMARA WAS DELIGHTED TO GET THE JOB. IT CAME WITH A corner office and all the bells and whistles of being a senior attorney at the firm. She even had an assistant and a paralegal. Tamara loved her new bright warm office with a fantastic view. Everything was like a dream to her until her first case fell across her desk. Tamara's first case with the firm would be to represent a controversial billionaire, Roderick Miles. Roderick Miles was also an Olympic gold medalist. Tamara was expected to not only take on the case but win it because Roderick was due to defend his skiing title. He couldn't do that if he was found guilty of sexual assault.

This was just great! Tamara sighed. "My trial by fire." She muttered, going over the case.

The evidence against Roderick Miles seemed pretty damning, and Tamara could see why his previous long list of attorneys had suggested him to plea out. But the firm expected her to go the whole nine yards and score the win for the man. Tamara couldn't help but feel that it was her destiny to defend scumbags. She sighed as she started wading through the files on Roderick Miles's case. Her assistant had set up a meeting between her and Roderick for the next day. That didn't give Tamara a lot of time to play catch up on his case.

—•⊙⊙·⊙⊙•—

"HELLO, MR. STEELE," one of the law firm's senior partners representing Roderick greeted him over the phone. "We'd like to inform you that we are pleased to have brought Miss Tamara Decker on board. She'd already applied for the position before you recommended her to us."

"It looks like it was meant to be," Roderick couldn't stop the grin that spread across his lips.

"I do have to warn you, though," the man told Roderick, "Miss Decker lost her last three cases, and her clients were convinced it was because she had sided with the other side."

"I've read her files," Roderick told the man. "I can't say I blame her if she did defect on those cases. They were pretty brutal, and those companies got what they deserved."

"I agree, but she's an attorney, and her loyalty needs to be her client," the man warned Roderick. "There is some pretty hard evidence against you, Mr. Steele, as we discussed when you came to us with your case."

"I trust Miss Decker will do what's right," Roderick defended her. "It's because she sees both sides of the story that I think she's ideal for my case."

"As you wish," the man said. "We are delighted to have someone of her background on board. I hope she has her edge back, though. A lot of us lose that over time."

"I know," Roderick sighed, knowing the man was referring to himself.

This particular senior partner had been relentless and had never lost a case. Until one day, his conscience had got the better of him. The man had let the other side win because the man knew it was the right thing to do.

Roderick knew this particular partner would've been the one to champion for Tamara to join the firm. That's why Roderick had asked him to find out if they could coax Tamara to work for them. Because Tamara had already applied for a job at the firm, Roderick knew fate was pushing them together.

Tamara's assistant phoned Roderick a day later to set up an appointment for him and Tamara to meet. However, he'd insisted that it be at his place, claiming he was wary of venturing out into public these days.

—•❦•❦•—

TAMARA SAT in the coffee shop, checking her watch. Where was he? It was so typical of him to be late. She had a meeting to get to and shouldn't have agreed to meet today. Tamara was about to leave when Zach rushed into the cafe.

"I'm sorry I'm late," Zach put his phone and keys on the table in front of him. "You're looking great." He smiled at Tamara as he sat down.

"Thank you," Tamara eyed Zach wearily. "I was surprised to hear from you after almost three months of silence."

"I needed to get my head straight," Zach told Tamara. "I want you to know there was not a day that went by that I didn't think of you."

"All you had to do was call," Tamara was not going to allow herself to fall for his flowery words.

"You don't know how many times I thought about it," Zach reached out to cover her hand with his, but Tamara pulled away.

"Why now, Zach?" Tamara's eyes narrowed suspiciously.

"Have you got a new case?" Zach looked at the folders in front of Tamara.

"You know I can't discuss that with you," Tamara put her phone over the top folder.

"I heard that you've moved to a new law firm," Zach smiled at her.

"I did," Tamara nodded. "I've just started, and I'm going to need to get going in a few minutes." She looked pointedly at her watch.

"Of course," Zach's phone bleeped. He saw the name and tried to cover it up quickly.

Tamara had seen the name on the phone and some of the messages. It was someone named Stella reminding him to get a few things before he came home.

"Who's Stella, Zach?" Tamara asked him coolly.

"Oh, a friend," Zach put his hand over his phone. "I want to hear what you've been up to these past three months." He smiled. "I've missed you."

"I think you'd better take that," Tamara cocked her head. "You may need to pick up more things on your way home tonight."

Tamara looked at her watch. She was going to be late if she didn't leave now. Tamara started gathering her files and picked up her purse. Then, right on cue, her Uber messaged her.

"Wait," Zach clicked on the red button on his phone, ignoring the call. "We need to talk." He ran his hand through his hair. "I have missed you, Tamara." He said softly, looking into her eyes.

"I don't believe that for a minute, Zach," Tamara paid her bill and stood up with her files and phone in hand. "I'm sure you and Stella have been too busy playing house to remember I exist." She looked at him coldly. "Why did you want me today Zach?"

"I told you," Zach breathed, "I wanted to see you."

"Sure you did," Tamara shook her head. "I think, as usual, you have an ulterior motive." Then it dawned on her, did he know who she was representing? Zach was a top reporter for a top News television station in LA.

"I have to go."

She turned and stalked out of the cafe, leaving Zach sitting staring after her. It felt good getting up and walking off when he obviously needed something from her. What an ass! Tamara thought as she climbed into the Uber and gave the driver the address.

EIGHT

A Cruel Twist of Fate

SHE DID HER BEST TO PULL HERSELF TOGETHER WHEN THEY pulled into the intimidating driveway that led to an even more intimidating house. She took a deep breath and cleared her mind while stepping out of the car and walking up to the front door. She rang the doorbell, trying to still her shaky hand.

A housekeeper answered the door and took Tamara through to a study. Tamara asked for water when the housekeeper asked if Tamara wanted something to drink. She looked at her watch. *Shit, she was seven minutes late!* Her new boss had told her Roderick Miles hated people being late for appointments. *Relax; it's going to be okay.* You got this! Tamara took a deep calming breath.

"Miss Decker?" a deep, eerily familiar voice said from behind her.

Tamara closed her eyes. *Please let it be someone with a similar voice!* She pleaded with her guardian angel. Slowly Tamara turned around, and her eyes met the eyes of the man who she'd bumped into in Mammoth Mountain.

"You're Roderick Miles?" Tamara's brows furrowed.

"And you're my mysterious next-door neighbor from the ski resort," Roderick smiled. "What a small world."

"It seems to be," Tamara gave Roderick a tight smile. She glanced at her watch. "I do apologize for being late."

"It was your first time coming to my home," Roderick drawled. "It was to be expected." He walked into his office and gestured for Tamara to sit in a chair in front of his desk. "I should've guessed you were a lawyer the first time you bowled me over." He took a seat in front of her.

"I guessed you were some sort of celebrity right away," Tamara told him. "You had that entitled air about you." She gave him a smug smile.

"I did know you were not a very good skier, though," Roderick smiled back at her. "I hope you managed to improve during your lessons during your stay at the resort."

"Mr. Steele," Tamara sighed. "If my job didn't depend on me defending you and doing everything I can to clear your name, I'd probably have walked out the moment I knew it was you."

"Honesty," Roderick raised his eyebrows. "I like that."

"I would prefer you kept our history out of our business relationship," Tamara said. "I hope we can get over what happened on the airplane and at the ski resort."

Roderick frowned at her. He was about to say something when she cut him off.

"If you are uncomfortable with me taking your case," Tamara cleared her throat, "I ask that you let my bosses know it had nothing to do with my capabilities as a lawyer."

Roderick sat staring at her for a few seconds as if he was contemplating what she'd said.

"I have no problem working with you, Tamara," Roderick deliberately used her first name. "But I have a few conditions to this partnership."

"How did you know my name?" Tamara looked at him curiously, not remembering having introduced herself to him.

"Your assistant told me your name when you called me," Roderick lied.

"Of course," Tamara gave him a tight smile, but he was not buying it.

Something had flickered in his eyes when he mentioned how he knew her name. Tamara had interrogated enough people in her career to know when someone wasn't telling the truth. And that was the second time Roderick Miles had not told her the truth in the short space of time she'd been here. So it was not a very good start for Tamara in believing his side of the story for his case.

"My conditions for our working arrangement," Roderick smiled at her, reminding Tamara of the Cheshire cat.

"Why do I get the feeling I'm not going to like them?" Tamara looked Roderick in the eye.

Roderick had gorgeous eyes that illuminated his gorgeous face, Tamara noted before giving herself a mental shake. She had no business noting how handsome or sexy the man was. Besides, Roderick was being accused of sexual assault from more than one woman. There was no way she'd put her trust in this man.

"If you want information about me, you will need to come to dinner with me at my request," Roderick pulled a card from his cardholder on his desk. He took out a pen and wrote a number on the back. "That's my personal phone number." He handed the card to her.

"I suppose I can agree to the dinner terms," Tamara told him, trying to tamper down the feeling of excitement of having dinner that sparked through her system.

"Great," Roderick leaned forward.

"Now, can we get started discussing your case?" Tamara opened the first folder in front of her. "You were accused of spiking the drinks of two different women on two different occasions."

"I can assure you that is false," Roderick said immediately. "I do not need to subdue a woman with drugs to get her to sleep with me." He said rather cockily.

"Maybe you felt like you were losing your touch?" Tamara raised her eyebrows seeing his cheeks get stained with an angry red. "Sometimes a little nudge in the right direction. Or maybe you get off on having your way with women who can't fight back?"

"I beg your pardon?" Roderick's eyes blazed with anger at her accusations. "I DO NOT now, nor DID I EVER, have to use drugs to have sex with a woman. I can have my pick, and I prefer my woman responsive to every touch of my fingers and tongue…." His mouth lifted in a half-smile as he noticed his words raise the tiny hairs on her arm.

"It took me under a minute to goad you into losing your cool and bring out your ego," Tamara looked at him. "Any lawyer worth their salt is going to know how big your ego is, and they're going to play on that. I'm your lawyer and on your side, and look how you responded to my accusations."

"That was cruel," Roderick hissed at her.

"No," Tamara shook her head, "that is what any lawyer worth their salt is going to do. They need to show off that big ego of yours."

"Well played," Roderick's eyes narrowed in on her.

"You have to remember that when you're on that stand, you're the prey, and the lawyer is the hunter," Tamara told him. "Unless you want to plead out and accept that fate, you need to learn to control that overinflated ego of yours."

"Noted," Roderick looked at her, a little taken aback by how harsh she'd been.

"It's not only when you're in court either," Tamara pulled her tablet out of her purse and searched for press releases about Roderick Miles. Which if she had done earlier, she would've known who he was. "Here," She typed in some media news about Roderick his previous lawyers had flagged.

"What am I looking at?" Roderick asked her as she hit play.

"This is a press release your previous lawyer flagged," Tamara told him. "I'm sorry I never got around to watching it. But in it, he said you got aggressive, arrogant, and defensive."

"I remember this," Roderick looked at the video. "I was accosted coming out of a restaurant. A whole lot of reporters were shoving their mics in my face."

"Wow," Tamara shook her head. "You love to rub in how you don't need to drug a woman with shit to get them into your bed."

"It's true," Roderick shrugged. "It doesn't matter who you are or what you look like. But, when you have money, things seem to fall into your lap."

"That attitude right there has to stop," Tamara warned him. "I would use your hugely inflated ego to bury you if I was on the other side of this case."

"Are you sure you want to take my case?" Roderick's eyes narrowed.

"Once I have taken your case, you do not have to question my loyalty," Tamara told him. "But I need you to follow my rules when it comes to your case." She advised him. "If you want to clear your name and reclaim both your company and right to compete. You'll listen to me, or you'll lose. It's up to you."

"Point taken," Roderick stared at her. "I think out of the queue of lawyers I've had; you may just be the one to win this thing for me."

"I'm not the one who is going to win this for you, Mr. Steele," Tamara corrected him. "I'm merely the driver on this journey. It's up to you where you're going to go. But I'm warning you again. If you don't follow my suggestions, you are going to lose."

"I promise to adhere to your suggestion if you promise to call me Roderick and not Mr. Steele," Roderick told her.

"Fine, Roderick," Tamara took her table back and looked at her watch. "I'm going to have to go. My ride should be here in two minutes." She gathered up her things. "I'll be in contact with you to go over a few things before your first court appearance."

"Would you like to have some lunch?" Roderick asked her.

"No, thank you," Tamara told Roderick coolly. "I have a meeting."

—•❁❁•❁❁•—

RODERICK WATCHED Tamara get in the Uber and drive away. She intrigued him. Tamara wasn't like any other woman he'd met before. She was even more beautiful than he'd remembered her to be. Roderick couldn't hide a pleased smile. He was going to enjoy this partnership. In a few short sentences, Tamara completely derailed Roderick and showed him just how good a lawyer she was.

No wonder he's not been able to intimidate her at the resort. She was probably used to facing down tougher nuts than Roderick. Tamara also had no idea who he was before now, and even now that she knew, she was unimpressed. In fact, he could've sworn she looked at him with utter disdain. At least it wasn't only Roderick that she felt contempt for, it was high profile people in general, or at least that was the impression he'd got.

Roderick sighed. He was going to enjoy getting to know the fiery Tamara Decker.

NINE

Tread With Caution

TAMARA HAD STARTED DIGGING INTO RODERICK'S LIFE. HE came from a comfortable middle-class family. He had two brothers, and both his parents were still alive. Roderick's love of ice-skating and skiing took him to compete first as a part of a double-figure skating team. Roderick and his partner had won many championships and were set to be the following Olympic gold medalists.

At the same time, Roderick's skiing had taken off, and he couldn't do both sports, so Roderick quit ice-skating for skiing. His skiing had won him two gold medals since the age of twenty. Roderick wanted to defend his title at the next winter Olympics. Unfortunately, he wouldn't be allowed to compete, and he'd probably be scratched from the Olympics altogether if his name wasn't cleared. In addition, his company had suspended him until after the verdict.

Tamara sighed. A lot was riding on this case and her winning it. Roderick's case was a high-profile one. Tamara's name would be linked to Roderick Miles after the first court appearance. All eyes would be on her and how she presents his case. The media coverage for a case like this was nothing like it was at her last company. Tamara's bosses had already warned her that the media would hunt her down and try to get tidbits about the case.

Tamara had grown up with a high-profile father. Luckily, he kept his home life private as her mother had been a pediatric neurosurgeon. She didn't need to be in the spotlight or have it shine on her patients, who were all minors. But still, that didn't stop the media from trying to hound their family. Even now that Tamara's father was retired, he still ran into some enthusiastic reporters wanting to make a quick buck. Before her father had become a judge or the Chief Justice of California, he'd tried some pretty high-profile cases that had rocked America. Now and then, someone would dredge those cases up to make a new headline with them.

Tamara had also learned from her father to scratch deeper than the surface. There were always two sides to a story. So far, all Tamara had read were the victims' sides. What was jangling alarm bells to Tamara was that both women had said almost the exact same thing in their interviews. It sounded rehearsed to Tamara. The women were sisters, and they had an older brother. With Nicole's help, Tamara had plans to have a coincidental meeting with the sister's brother that night at the man's favorite hangout. Another part of the sister's story that didn't make sense to Tamara was why, after the first sister said Roderick had sexually assaulted her, did the second sister go near him? The sisters hadn't been sexually assaulted on the same night. It had happened three days apart.

The sisters alleged that they were at the same resort Roderick was staying in. The first sister had met Roderick in the resort bar. They'd chatted, and he'd bought her dinner, after which they'd gone to a local club where

Roderick and the woman had danced and had fun. Roderick had asked her to come back to his room, but she'd refused. He'd coaxed her to have a nightcap with him in the hotel lounge. The woman had said the famous skier so enthralled her that she'd gone and had the nightcap. Roderick had asked the woman to get them a table while he ordered their drinks. The woman said that must've been when he'd spiked her drink. After a few sips of her drink, she started to feel dizzy.

Roderick had helped her up and said he'd take her to her room. Instead, Roderick took the woman to his room, not hers, where he'd proceeded to have his way with her. *His way with her?* Tamara frowned. *Who the hell spoke like that in the twenty-first century?* Her sister had told nearly the exact same story right down to Roderick having his way with her after he'd drugged her. Once the news had hit the tabloids, four other women had come forward alleging that Roderick had done the same thing to them. The woman alleged that they'd been paid off to keep quiet about what had happened.

Tamara shook her head. Nearly all the stories were the same. Meeting Roderick at a bar, having dinner with him, dancing with him, and then the nightcap led to rape. Something about all this didn't sit right with Tamara, and her instincts were telling her there was a lot more going on here than first met the eye. Two people, Roderick's previous attorneys, were looking for to question had mysteriously vanished. They were two witnesses that were the key to Roderick's case. *So, where the hell were they?* Something in the lawyers who were on this case before her notes caught her attention. She frowned and laid each lawyer's notes out in front of her.

That couldn't be a coincidence. Tamara thought, chewing the tip of her pen. She picked up her phone and called the only private detective she trusted. Tamara needed him to dig into another name that kept popping up in the case notes. This name popped up a lot right before Roderick's former lawyers told him to plead guilty. Tamara also needed her private investigator to check for any activity that could point to the other lawyers being bribed or coerced into getting Roderick to plead guilty. Flashes of sexy eyes roving her body and the feel of a solid chest beneath her fingers flashed through her mind. *No, Tamara, you can't become involved with Roderick Miles in any way. No matter how sexy he is.*

"YOU KNOW I can't discuss the case with you," Tamara said to Nicole as they headed for the bar where the sisters accusing Roderick of sexual assault hung out. "But I can tell you there's more to this story than meets the eye."

"It's good to see you back in the groove of things, Tamara," Nicole looked worriedly at Tamara. "But you need to tread carefully with this case. It's a hot potato. All eyes are on this case. I have to tell you that Roderick's company just employed my firm to represent them."

"Why would Roderick take his company's business to another law firm?" Tamara asked Nicole, frowning.

"He didn't," Nicole told Tamara. "The new acting chairman of the company did."

"I wonder if Roderick knows about this." Tamara's brain started to tick over.

"You need to be very careful with this case, Tamara," Nicole shook her head worriedly. "You also need to keep as much distance as possible between you and your client."

"What's that supposed to mean?" Tamara frowned at Nicole.

"You have that look every time you say his name," Nicole raised her eyebrows.

"What look?" Tamara glared at Nicole. "I'm just trying to figure out what is going on. But, unfortunately, there are some things about this case that are not adding up. I need to have all the information to defend *my client!*"

"Okay," Nicole held up her hands. "We're here."

"Are you ready?" Tamara looked at Nicole. "We've not done this in a while." She grinned.

"I must say that I do miss our undercover missions," Nicole grinned back. "I have my tablet at the ready." She held up the device.

"Is your wedding ring off," Tamara glanced at Nicole's finger.

"All gone and lines covered up," Nicole held up her hand.

"Let's do this," Tamara breathed, opening the door to the bar.

Tamara and Nicole walked into the bar with Nicole watching something on her tablet.

"Target acquired," Tamara said softly. "He's exactly where the PI said he'd be."

"Don't sound so disappointed," Nicole looked up from the tablet covertly.

"It's just sad that someone could be such a creature of habit," Tamara sighed. "You need to be on my left."

Tamara and Nicole swapped sides as they walked over to the bar.

"I can't wait to go to Salt Lake," Nicole said excitedly, watching the video on her notepad. She was supposedly not looking where she was going. "I want to win the competition to go bobsledding with Roderick Miles."

Nicole walked into their target's chair.

"Oh, shit," Nicole dropped her tablet but turned to

apologize to the man. "I'm so sorry." She fumbled around the man.

"I'm fine," the man gave Nicole a tight smile. He got off his chair to help Nicole retrieve her tablet and froze, noticing the video playing on it. "Are you watching skiing videos of Roderick Miles?" His eyes narrowed as he handed the tablet back to Nicole.

"Well, yes," Nicole took her tablet. "We're hoping to go to Salt Lake to win the bobsledding with Roderick Miles competition."

"She's trying to go to Salt Lake to win the bobsledding competition," Tamara told the man. "I'm going there to ski. I don't want my name tied to that man's name." Tamara ordered a drink for her and Nicole. "Can I get you a drink as an apology for my short-sighted friend?" She glared at Nicole.

"Oh, come now," Nicole gave Tamara a dreamy look. "You can't believe everything you read in the news. Besides, he's so dreamy and an Olympic gold medalist." She sighed. "I have to go to the ladies." She put her table on the counter. "I'm sorry I bumped into you." She apologized to the man once again.

"No damage done," the man gave her another tight smile.

"She doesn't mean any harm," Tamara sighed. "She's always been a skiing fan and has done the sport competitively herself." She explained.

"Ah," the man nodded. "That would explain her short-sightedness when it comes to that prick Roderick Miles."

"So I take it, like me, you're not a fan?" Tamara was about to pay the bartender but looked at the man. "Can I buy you a drink?"

"Sure, why not?" The man's eyes traveled over Tamara.

Tamara suppressed a shudder of disgust. There was something sinister about the man. He was the type of man Tamara would not leave her to drink around. However, she had to hold her disgust in check because she needed answers from the man.

"You should tell your friend that Roderick Miles does take advantage of drugged women," the man told Tamara after his third drink with her. "I know because it was my sisters that he drugged. I also know he's done it plenty of times before."

"I'm sorry to hear about your sisters," Tamara said, "but you really should be careful talking about the man like this. You never know who's listening to you." She warned him.

"Shit, I don't care," he downed his shot and ordered another, offering Tamara one, but she declined. "The man's a dick and deserves what's coming for him."

"You really don't like Roderick Miles, do you?" Tamara twirled the stem of her wine glass.

"Hate the guy," the man said. "You'd think his leeching lawyers would at least offer my sisters something for their suffering. But the bastard wants to go to trial because he thinks he can get away with anything. He has a huge surprise coming. Those other women will have him over the barrel. They know how to get him."

"What do you mean?" Tamara frowned when he told her exactly what the other women were going to say in court. *How did this man know those women's testimonies?* Only their lawyers and Tamara knew that. "Again, I don't think you should be discussing this in a bar."

"Bullshit," the man said with venom in his voice. "The world needs to know what that bastard is really like." He started to laugh. "Do you want to know a secret?"

"Aren't you worried you're going to get in trouble for

talking about this to a complete stranger?" Tamara asked him.

"Hell no," he shook his head. "I wish I could say this to his Goddamn soul-sucking lawyers," he spat.

Tamara was shocked at the following words out of the man's mouth. Luckily Nicole reappeared from a bogus phone call, and they left. Tamara made sure she'd got everything recorded as she went home.

TEN

A Working Dinner

RODERICK HAD INVITED TAMARA FOR DINNER TO DISCUSS her progress on his case. She knew she should've insisted on him meeting her at her office or have a Skype call. Especially after the evidence was piling up against him. Tamara didn't believe the sisters who'd started this whole thing or their brother at all. The man clearly had a grudge against Roderick, and she'd found out some fascinating information about him from her PI.

"You look lovely," Roderick answered the door this time. "Come in."

"Thank you," Tamara smiled at him and walked past him. "You have a lovely home."

"Thank you," Roderick led her into the lounge. "I thought we could have a glass of wine before dinner."

"Sure," Tamara walked into the modern but cozy lounge and chose an armchair.

Roderick had a bottle of wine on the table that he had not opened and two glasses. Tamara tried not to look at them suspiciously. But Roderick picked up her discomfort.

"Follow me," Roderick picked up the glasses and bottle of wine.

Tamara frowned, got up, and followed Roderick. He led her through the gorgeous kitchen, where he introduced her to his chef.

"Here, Mike," Roderick gave Mike the bottle of wine. "You can have this. It's not to my guests' liking."

Mike looked quite taken aback.

"I'm sorry, Miss Decker," Mike told her. "Would you like me to choose another?"

"No thanks, Mike," Roderick told him and walked Tamara into a rather impressive wine cellar. "Pick any bottle you like."

"I'm sorry, Roderick," Tamara sighed.

"No," Roderick shook his head. "I understand. You don't know me that well, and you've obviously gone through all the case files."

Tamara wandered over to a rack and chose a bottle of Merlot.

"Good choice," Roderick smiled. "Now, if you step back into the kitchen, you can get glasses off the shelf."

"May I open that for you?" Mike offered.

"Thank you," Tamara was feeling bad by the time they were back in the lounge.

"I take it you've made some headway into my case," Roderick sipped his wine.

"I have," Tamara nodded. "I do have a lot of questions for you." She told him. "Starting with your side of the story."

"Isn't it all in your files?" Roderick asked.

"I would still like to hear the story from you," Tamara told him.

"How about we get to know each other first?" Roderick

smiled. "I'm sure after a hard day of work, you need to unwind a little."

Tamara felt regretful for not trusting him with the wine, so she let him turn the conversation away from the case. She'd get him to talk about a little in the evening.

As the evening went on, Tamara found herself relaxing, and she'd enjoyed the meal his chef had prepared for them. She now knew more about Roderick's family. He had a brother and an older half-brother that was four when his mother married his father. Roderick wasn't as close as he should be to his family. Roderick would not discuss with Tamara, especially after Roderick's parents had sided with his half-brother in matters.

They'd watched a few of Roderick's skiing and ice-skating videos. Every time Tamara asked Roderick a question about the case, he found a way to change the subject. He was deliberately evasive, and she didn't understand why when he so clearly needed her to win this case for him. She was getting so annoyed with Roderick that when he started to ask questions about her, she found ways to avoid answering them.

They were into their second bottle of wine when Tamara started to feel a little strange and light-headed. She needed some air, and maybe it was time to get home. Tamara could help wonder if Roderick had somehow managed to spike her drink then shook the idea off. She was his lawyer. Tamara was sure he wouldn't be that stupid or reckless as to drug and try to take advantage of his lawyer. As if on cue, her phone rang. It was Zach. *Why was he phoning so late?* Tamara looked at her watch. It was just after eleven in the evening.

"Excuse me," Tamara stood up with her phone. "I have to take this call."

Tamara tried not to wobble or stumble as she made her way into the hall.

"Zach?" Tamara answered the phone.

"Hi," Zach's voice sounded like he was drunk. "I had to call to tell you, you really are looking great, and I miss you so much."

"This is not the time for this, Zach," Tamara said into the phone. "I'm currently in a late business meeting."

"We need to talk," Zach told her. "Please tell me we can meet to talk. Maybe you can come over to my place sometime soon."

"I'm sorry, Zach," Tamara sailed coolly, "but I have to go."

Tamara hung up. Maybe he hadn't been after Roderick's story after all. Zach had tried to call her a few times since their meeting at the cafe. Zach had also left her a few text messages, which she had chosen to ignore. Tamara sighed and turned around to see Roderick walking out of the lounge.

"Do you need to go?" Roderick looked pointedly at her phone.

"Yes," Tamara gave him a small smile. "I do." She walked through to the lounge and picked up her light coat and purse. "I've had a great evening. Thank you, Roderick, but I have a lot of work tomorrow."

"I've called my chauffeur," Roderick told her. "He'll take you home."

"I was going to call an Uber," Tamara smiled.

"No need," Roderick assured her. "I also had a nice time. Thank you for coming."

Roderick walked Tamara out onto the terrace, and they waited for the chauffeur to pull up in a black town car.

"I do need to talk to you about your side of the story

before the court case," Tamara told Roderick when he walked her to the car.

"Let me know a date, and I'll make a plan," Roderick smiled at her, opening the car door.

"Great, I'll have my assistant contact you," Tamara slid into the back seat.

"No," Roderick shook his head. "I would rather you called me." His eyes locked with hers when he ducked down to speak to her. "I had a good time." His voice was deep and husky. "Good night, Tamara. Sweet dreams."

Roderick broke eye contact when he stood, making Tamara feel strangely cold. Tamara watched Roderick walk up the stairs and into his house without looking back as the car drove down the long tree-lined driveway.

—•◦◯◦·◦◯◦•—

RODERICK WAS FEELING A LITTLE LIGHT-HEADED. Which was strange because all he'd been drinking that night was club soda. Roderick shook it off and put it down to him, being tired and stressed out over who the board had chosen as the company's acting Chairman. Roderick was still smarting at how quickly they'd replaced him as the head of his own damn company.

Roderick had started Spirit Gear, sinking all his hard-earned money and sponsorship funds into the company. For the first five years, he'd hardly seen a return as he was determined only to have to borrow the barest minimum for the rest. Roderick never should've taken the bad advice he did because now he'd lost control of his company. When this damn court case was over, Roderick would start again, and this time he would run the company the way he saw fit.

Roderick was no one's fool. He'd been putting money

away for many years. He had more than enough to use as startup capital and still live comfortably. Roderick would not make the same mistakes a second time. Roderick had been burned badly, but the one thing it had taught him was who he could and couldn't trust. It was a sad day when the ones closest to you were the ones plunging the knife into your back.

Roderick had a shower and drank a lot of water, trying to clear his foggy head. Roderick had a restless night as he had the weirdest dreams about someone trying to get into his room and telling him he needed to sign some papers. He could remember telling them to go to hell and then telling him he's not signing anything his lawyer hasn't checked over. That's when Tamara popped into his dreams, and the tempo changed to a hot steamy one.

ELEVEN

One Step Ahead

"THOMAS," TAMARA KNOCKED ON HER BOSS'S DOOR, "DO you have a minute to discuss Roderick Miles's case?"

"Of course," Thomas invited her into his office. "Come in and take a seat."

"I'm worried about the case," Tamara admitted to Thomas. "I don't have enough evidence to work with." She pinched the bridge of her nose. "He is also evasive about his side of the story."

"Use whatever means you need to get the evidence you require," Thomas sat back in his seat, fiddling with his pen. "Roderick's big weakness is women."

"I'm not sure what that has to do with getting the information I need," Tamara frowned at Thomas. "I have a few more people to find."

"Good, good," Thomas nodded. "You are doing well, Tamara. We are impressed with your progress."

"Thank you," Tamara smiled. "I have a meeting, so I'd better go. Thank you for listening, Thomas."

"Anytime, and keep me updated," Thomas waved Tamara out of his office.

Tamara breathed. Why did she feel that not many people thought she had a chance of winning this case? It was like everyone she'd talked to believed Roderick to be guilty. That didn't make Tamara feel good at all. Was she only given this case to appease Roderick and because they didn't have much confidence in her ability to win it? Did they want Roderick to lose?

Tamara walked back to her office, deep in thought. There was something she was missing. Even though all the evidence was there, it didn't fit together somehow. Tamara did find Roderick extremely attractive, and she had to agree that he didn't need to drug a woman to have sex with them. From everything she'd seen of him so far and the women, he had dated. Roderick dated strong, independent women. Not shrinking violets. With an ego the size he had, she doubted he'd want his women to be unresponsive.

Tamara had to get Roderick to tell her his side of the story. She also needed to find out if any money was transferred to the woman who had allegedly been paid off.

Tamara rushed into her office, noting the time. She would be late to meet with her private detective, who had some information for her about the two sisters. She nearly died of fright when Zach jumped up from the chair in her office he'd been waiting in.

"Zach!" Tamara breathed, holding her chest. "What on earth are you doing here?"

"I came to ask you to lunch," Zach held out a bright bouquet for her. "I really need to talk to you. I've missed you so much."

"I can't," Tamara told him.

Tamara walked around her desk and opened her drawer to take out her purse, which she strung over her arm. She dropped all of Roderick's files into her briefcase.

Tamara wasn't risking anyone tampering with the information she'd gathered.

Tamara didn't want to seem paranoid, but she'd sworn she'd seen Carl leaving her office a few times since she took over Roderick's case. When she'd asked her assistant, the woman had lied to her face and said she never let Carl into Tamara's office. When Tamara was back from her meeting, she wanted to talk to HR about replacing the woman. Tamara wanted to bring in her assistant that had left when she did. She worked well with her old assistant.

"Tamara?" Zach snapped Tamara out of her deep thought. "You did one of your zoning out things again. Are you working on a big case?"

And there it was! Tamara thought. Zach was fishing. *Had he somehow found out the case she was working?* She frowned at him.

"What do you know about the case I'm working on?" Tamara asked Zach suspiciously.

"Nothing," Zach's brows furrowed together. "Why? Should I know something about it?"

"No," Tamara shook her head. "Now, if you don't mind, I need to leave and lock my office."

"Will you have dinner with me tonight?" Zach asked hopefully as Tamara ushered him out of her office.

"Sorry, Zach," Tamara locked her office door behind her. She'd had the locks changed early that morning, and she was the only one with a key. "I have plans tonight, and I'm busy for the rest of the week."

"Come on, Tamara," Zach followed her to the elevator. "Can you look me in the eye and tell me you haven't missed me?"

Tamara pushed the down button and turned towards Zach. "Honestly, Zach, I've been too busy picking up the pieces of my life and trying to stick them back together again to miss you."

"I deserved that," Zach said, stepping into the elevator with her when it arrived. "How are you getting to your meeting?" He asked her as the elevator zoomed down to the ground floor. "Let me give you a lift that will give us some time to talk."

"I'm being fetched," Tamara told him. She stepped out of the elevator, immediately spotting the driver waiting for her. "Now, if you'll excuse me, my ride's here. Please call before you come calling again." She started walking away, saying over her shoulder. "Goodbye, Zach."

—•ᏄᎧ·ᎧᏄ•—

"ARE YOU HAVING FUN?" Nicole walked over to Tamara and handed her a fresh glass of wine.

"If you mean by fun, am I constantly being hit on by every single or cheating scumbag here, fun." Tamara sighed and took the glass of wine Nicole offered her. "It's been a crazy month, and I have the first court appearance the day after tomorrow. So I can't stay late."

"I'm glad you came. I know how busy you are with this case," Nicole smiled. "But our anniversary party wouldn't have been the same without you here." She hugged Tamara. "I'm sorry about Elias's scumbag friends."

"It's okay. I can handle them," Tamara grinned. "I wish you'd chosen a different venue. You know that this is Zach's favorite haunt."

No sooner had Tamara said Zach's name when he walked through the door. Alone. He immediately scanned the room, looking for Tamara.

"Don't be mad," Nicole told Tamara. "Well, actually, you can't be mad with me because it's my anniversary, and remember our pact to never be mad at each other on a special day."

"We were ten when we made that pact," Tamara told Nicole. "What did you do?"

"Please hear Zach out," Nicole pleaded with Tamara. "I know what he did was stupid. Men do stupid things. It's in their nature. But I believe he loves you, and I think you make a great couple."

"Nicole, you had no right to interfere with this," Tamara hissed. "I told you I was over him."

"If you say so," Nicole squinted. "But I don't believe you. I've seen that deep soulful look in your eyes lately. You get like that when you're down or in love, and you've been this way since your breakup with Zach."

"You're wrong, Nicole," Tamara hissed, but before she could say anymore, Zach approached.

To Tamara's utter mortification, Zach didn't say a word but dropped down on one knee and pulled out a small blue box.

"Tamara Decker, I love you, and I know I was a complete jerk, but I'm nothing without you," Zach popped the box open to reveal the most beautiful ring. "Will you marry me?"

Tamara's head started to spin, and her heartbeat was like a drum in her chest. She looked around the room that suddenly seemed distorted. She felt hot, and her chest was tight.

"Tamara?" Nicole gave her a curious look. "What do you say?" She leaned over and whispered in Tamara's ear. "Please say yes."

Tamara's eyes flew to meet Nicole's. She felt a pressure headache start to build up her spine. Then, when her head stopped spinning, she noted that the room had gone quiet, and all eyes were now on her.

"Tamara?" Zach looked up at her. "Come on, honey. You can't leave me hanging here."

"I…" Tamara croaked, swallowed down her entire glass of one, and cleared her throat. "No." She shook her head. "No, I can't marry you, Zach, and you should've spoken to me before you came here and made a spectacle out of both of us."

Tamara grabbed her purse and jacket from the table and stormed out of the cocktail lounge through a sea of gaping spectators.

—•◦◯◦•◯◦•—

TAMARA WAS EXHAUSTED. All she wanted to do was go home, order Chinese take-out, have a bath, and then relax in front of the TV with her food. The court case had gone well, and Tamara had managed to discredit the four women who'd accused Roderick of paying them off to keep quiet about the sexual assault. Tamara wasn't able to use any of the conversations she'd had with the sister's brother when she'd met him in the bar. But her assistants had found a paper trail and connection between the brother and the four other women. The evidence against those four women and their association with the sister's brother was also enough to cast doubt on the sister's story.

As Tamara let herself into her apartment, her phone rang. It was Nicole. Tamara had been ignoring Nicole's calls and messages since the night of Nicole's wedding anniversary. She'd also been avoiding Zach's calls and messages. Tamara's office looked like a flower shop. Zach had sent her many bunches of flowers.

Why wasn't he getting the message? Tamara sighed. She'd just hung up from ordering her take-out when Roderick phoned.

"Hi," Roderick greeted her when she answered. "I was wondering if you wanted to have dinner with me to celebrate how well court went today."

"Sorry, Roderick," Tamara sighed. "But not tonight. I'm glad we seemed to have won this round, but there are a few more to go."

"I'd like to take this win," Roderick told her enthusiastically. "It gives me hope that we could win this after all."

"Yes," Tamara said. "We could. I need more cooperation from you, though."

"Fine, have dinner with me, and you'll have my full cooperation," Roderick gave her a boyish grin.

"I can't, not tonight," Tamara said. "I must go. Have a good evening." She hung up the phone.

Tamara's food had arrived, and she'd dished it up, ready to eat after her bath. She was about to get undressed when her phone rang. She looked at the number and frowned. The line went dead, and a text message appeared a few seconds later. Her eyes widened. It was a call she'd been waiting for. Her phone rang again, and Tamara answered it. She listened to the caller as she grabbed her jacket, keys, and purse. When she hung up, she stepped out into the night to find a car waiting for her.

TWELVE

The Wrong Side

Tamara was starting to feel like a yo-yo of conflicting emotions. She'd been so excited to get hold of the person she'd been trying to track down. But what they had to say wasn't favorable for Roderick. It had put a lot of doubt in Tamara's mind as to Roderick's innocence. This morning she'd been contacted by the lawyer representing the four women who'd come forward to accuse Roderick of buying their silence.

Suddenly the two women she'd discredited the other day in court had the evidence they failed to produce before the court case. The lawyer wanted to have a meeting with only her, himself, and the two sisters accusing Roderick of rape. They didn't want Roderick present because it was too distressing for the women. It was bad enough they had to see him in court, the lawyer told her.

Tamara was so glad the other assistant had been assigned back to Carl, and her old assistant, as well as her paralegal from her old law firm, had been hired to help Tamara. Georgia was a great paralegal, and Sienna was the glue that kept Tamara together. She had been surprised when Thomas had told her she could hire both of them. Roderick Miles had told them to spare no expense when setting Tamara up with whatever help she needed.

"Georgia, Sienna, can I see you please?" Tamara called from her office door.

The two women got up and walked into Tamara's office.

"Did you get my message?" Georgia asked Tamara.

Georgia had been keeping her ear to the ground around the office because Tamara was sure someone was leaking information to the opposing attorney for Roderick's case. It was too coincidental to Tamara how the opposing attorney knew things that Tamara hadn't told anyone. Tamara was sure it was not Thomas because the man was named partner and wouldn't risk his reputation or partner-ship in one of the top law firms in LA. On the other hand, Carl was a disgruntled employee and, as far as Tamara could see, was living way above his means somehow. He'd recently bought himself a shiny new top-of-the-range Jaguar and was looking at a new house in an up-market suburb for him and his wife.

Tamara didn't want to accuse Carl outright of being paid by someone to feed them information. Maybe Carl did have a rich aunt who'd recently died and left him her fortune. Tamara hoped that was the truth, for Carl and his wife's sake. It was a serious offense leaking sensitive infor-mation to the opposition. Carl would never be able to practice law again. Tamara hoped that man hadn't let greed and anger at the firm make him do anything stupid.

"I did, thank you, Georgia," Tamara smiled at the older woman. "Can you get hold of our private detective to look into that for us, please?"

Tamara smiled at the blush that stained Georgia's cheeks. She was in her late thirties and divorced for three years after catching her husband cheating with a much younger woman. Georgia had thrown her life into her work and made sure Tamara's life ran like clockwork. She'd missed Georgia when she'd quit the previous law firm. Not long after Tamara had left, both Georgia and Sienna had left. Like Tamara, they'd struggled to find work. She was so glad she could help them and have her super-team back together.

"Where are we on tracking down the last two witnesses?" Tamara asked the women.

"I've managed to get an appointment with Roderick's mother," Georgia told Tamara. "Who do you want me to schedule to go see her?"

"Thank you," Tamara said, "Sienna, will you have time to go meet with Roderick's mother?"

"Yes," Sienna nodded. Tamara knew the young paralegal would make the time. Sienna was four years younger than Tamara. Working with Tamara had been her first job, and Sienna was thorough, tough, and loyal.

"Would Georgia be able to join me?" Sienna looked at Georgia, then at Tamara.

"I don't mind if Georgia doesn't," Tamara looked questioningly at Georgia.

"I love going on witness interviews," Georgia smiled at Sienna, "I'll make an appointment for us."

"Great," Sienna breathed a sigh of relief. "I feel much better when I have someone with me to make sure I don't miss anything."

"I do not doubt that you would never miss a thing," Tamara smiled encouragingly at Sienna.

Tamara understood why Sienna was double-checking and then triple-checking her work. She thought it was partly her fault Tamara had lost the three cases that had cost Tamara her job. Tamara had tried on many occasions to make Sienna understand those cases were not her fault. Sienna had done everything right.

"I need our PI to get working on Carl's information right away," Tamara told Georgia. "Sienna, I'm going to need to have the exhibits for the next court date to go over as soon as possible."

"I'll have them for you within the next day or two. I'm waiting on some more evidence to put the final touches to it," Sienna told Tamara.

"I'm going to need both of you with me tomorrow afternoon to meet the opposing council along with the six women accusing our client of sexual assault. They don't want Roderick in attendance," Tamara started to pack her files into her new briefcase. "Oh, Georgia, did you manage to transcribe the recording from my conversation last night?"

"I did," Georgia frowned, "I just find it a little too convenient that you found that witness, and then the very next day, the opposing counsel wants to meet you."

"I do too," Sienna's brows drew together. "I will do some more digging into that witness as well to make sure we know everything we can about them."

"What about all the other evidence that's suddenly come to light," Tamara breathed. "Those recordings of the incidents are pretty damning."

"And also a little too convenient," Sienna told Tamara. "This is the twenty-first century. It is easy to falsify a recording." She looked at Tamara. "If you don't mind me taking them to my fiancé. He can get over them for you. I'll write up the NDA's and sign him on board if you agree."

"I trust him," Tamara nodded. "I don't want to have to try to bury the evidence. That's not how we operate, but I'm not too sure this is evidence. It's more like a trap of some sorts."

"Like it's been handed to us to see if we will submit it or try to bury it?" Georgia shook her head. "I think we need to give it to Sienna to take to her tech genius fiancé."

"I agree," Tamara nodded. "Sienna, do you think he can get it done for us, like, yesterday? I have a feeling this goes a lot deeper than sexual assault. Something is going on that we're not seeing."

"I'll dig into all Roderick Miles's employees, colleagues, family members, and friends," Sienna told Tamara. "I've already started, to be honest."

"I'll help, Sienna," Georgia offered.

"Thank you," Tamara looked at her watch. "I'm so glad you are both with me again." She smiled at the two women who said they were so glad to be working with Tamara again. "Now, if you'll excuse me, I have to go meet with our client."

"Good luck," Georgia and Sienna chorused.

"Please lock up before you go," Tamara had managed to secure the double office next to hers for Georgia and Sienna to share.

"Will do," Georgia nodded.

Tamara ran out of the office. She knew Roderick was at home because Georgia had confirmed he was home all day. It was time to take off the kid gloves with Roderick. He needed to come clean. The person Tamara had met with had given her all the new evidence. They had told Tamara that Roderick had approached all of the women connected with the case. Apparently, he was trying to buy them off again. Tamara had been played a recording of

Roderick talking to one of the women over the phone. The voice had sounded like Roderick, but it was not conclusive evidence. To be fair, that could've been anyone impersonating Roderick. She needed hard evidence.

—•ೞ•ೞ•—

TAMARA SAW the surprise in Roderick's eyes when he answered the door to find her standing there. When Tamara saw him, she felt her throat go dry. He'd been swimming and was standing without a shirt on and a towel wrapped around his waist. His ripped torso was still glittering with droplets of water, as was his dark wet hair. Tamara swallowed, feeling embarrassed about staring at his amazing male body when her eyes met his, and he had a knowing smile on his face.

"This is a pleasant surprise," Roderick smiled sexily at Tamara. "Come in. Sorry, I'm not dressed for the occasion."

"It's fine," Tamara croaked and cleared her throat. "I'm sorry to drop in like this, but we need to talk about your case. I've come into possession of some damning evidence against you, and the opposing lawyer has requested a meeting with only me."

"Make yourself comfortable in the lounge," Roderick told her. "I'll go put some clothes on. Would you like something to drink?"

"No, thank you, I'm fine," Tamara assured him, taking a seat in an armchair.

Tamara was glad Roderick had left her alone for a few minutes. The same feeling of electricity that had zinged through her every time they met since that first unfortunate meeting zinged through her. Only this time, it was so intense she had to force herself not to lean forward and kiss away the water droplets running down his impressive chest. The man was as sexy as all hell. None of what was going on in this case made sense. Why would a man like Roderick Miles drug and rape women? Her gut was screaming at her that he was innocent but was that because she was attracted to him. Tamara needed to believe that? Her mind was still processing the evidence that she'd recently been given.

Tamara wanted to give Roderick the benefit of the doubt, but to do that, he needed to start talking to her. Today!

TAMARA SIGHED. She felt like she and Roderick had been talking in circles for hours. Roderick had told her something but nothing at the same time.

"I promise you I never tried to bribe or pay anyone off," Roderick assured her. "I won't even sign company papers without your approval. You know that."

"Did they remove the acting chairman?" Tamara asked Roderick.

Tamara had been so wrapped up in the case she'd not asked him what had happened to the acting Chairman, who Tamara had managed to discredit.

"Thanks to my beautiful, intelligent, and very cunning lawyer, the board isn't going to appoint anyone. I will still be consulted on company decisions," Roderick told her with a smile. "I've managed to right the ship. Thank you, Tamara."

When Tamara had found out that Jaylon Vance, the owner of Monolith Clothing Company, had been appointed as acting Chairman, she'd been surprised to find him at the head of his rival company, Spirit Gear. Jaylon had insisted that he was no longer part of Monolith Clothing Company. Tamara had simply reminded Jaylon that she knew where to look for his skeletons as his former lawyer. Monolith Clothing Company had been a client of her previous law firm.

Jaylon hadn't been happy with Tamara's threats, but he'd backed down and stepped down as acting chairman but not before warning her to watch her back. He had sneered that Roderick Miles wasn't the innocent victim she thought he was. Tamara was still a little unclear as to how Jaylon Vance managed even to get a foot in the door of Spirit Gear. She didn't have time to ponder on that right now. Tamara needed Roderick to start cooperating.

"Roderick, we need to prove you haven't been trying to pay off the women," Tamara told him while she was getting ready to leave. "Thank you for finally giving me something to work with."

Tamara was meeting Nicole for the first time since that fateful night when Zach had proposed to her.

"Why don't you stay for dinner," Roderick's eyes darkened as his eyes locked with hers.

"I can't," Tamara swallowed. "I have a prior engagement."

"Can't you cancel it?" Roderick's voice lowered when he stepped closer to her.

"I…" Tamara cleared her throat. His cologne teased her senses. The warmth of his body so close to hers was playing havoc on other parts of her body. "I really can't."

"Pity," Roderick whispered as his face lowered to hers.

Tamara stood mesmerized. Her heartbeat picked up, and her breathing became labored while butterflies fluttered in her stomach. His lips slowly came down towards hers. She wanted nothing more than to wrap her arms around his neck and pull his lips to hers. Instead, she stilled her wayward thoughts and took a step back.

"I have to go. My Uber's here," Tamara gave Roderick a tight smile. "I can see myself out."

Tamara turned and fled out the front door, thankful to see her Uber pulling up.

THIRTEEN

A Dinner Invitation

IT HAD BEEN ALMOST A WEEK SINCE RODERICK HAD LAST
seen Tamara. She'd sent either her paralegal or legal
assistant to their follow-up meetings. When he phoned, she
was never in the office or in a meeting. Tamara wasn't
answering any of his messages either. Roderick was getting
irritated. He was also angry with himself for being upset
and letting a woman get under his skin. The last time
Roderick had allowed a woman to get under his skin like
this, it had nearly destroyed him emotionally. He'd vowed
he'd never let another woman consume him like that ever
again.

Roderick might not be as innocent as he let on to be.
He'd been with his fair share of women after his heart had
been torn to shreds, and he'd almost lost everything.
Roderick was wary of women, especially lately. Most of
the women who'd accused Roderick of sexual assault he
wanted to say he'd never met them in his life. But truth be
told, he could've met them and had sex with them. After
his engagement ended, Roderick had gone on a bender.
Most nights, he was blind drunk and had blind drunk sex.

He can't remember how many telephone numbers he'd thrown away or promises he'd made to call but never did.

Out of the two sisters, Roderick could only remember the one, and his recollection of that night was completely different from hers. Only this time, Roderick knew he wasn't drunk. He'd stopped drinking and was sobering up. Roderick had to if he wanted to get into shape to ski again. His Lydia period was over, and he was back into full training. Roderick knew he should tell Tamara the truth, but he was hoping she'd figure it out. There were a few things he couldn't tell her for different reasons. He'd been subtly trying to point her in the right direction, but she was still heading in the wrong one. Maybe Roderick should send her some anonymous evidence himself. He wondered if he could find out who she'd hired as a private investigator to snoop around.

Roderick picked up the phone to call his contact, who was like a private investigator only so much better and had fingers in many handy pies. He needed to get some information to Tamara so that it didn't look like it was him. Roderick knew he was risking a lot, his whole Olympic career even. If he had to give that up, so be it. But Roderick wanted his company back and moved it in the direction it was supposed to go in. The way his company stood now with this scandal of his was bleeding money. Which gave a company, Monolith Clothing Company, that made knock-offs of his brand ground to gain.

Roderick was a play-it-by-the-book kind of guy. Especially when it came to his business, it had come as no surprise to him when he'd found out who the owners of Monolith Clothing Company were. When Roderick had approached the owners to have a showdown with them, they'd proposed an agreement. Roderick knew better than to get involved with Monolith Clothing Company's owners and turned down their offer.

The name of Monolith Clothing Company's products was also similar to his products' brand names. So much so that when Monolith Clothing Company's inferior product nearly killed a few people, Roderick's company was taken to court. Luckily Roderick's lawyers could prove that the product didn't belong to them and had the attention turn on the real culprits. Monolith Clothing Company nearly had to close down when they were taken to court. The company had to pull all of its top product lines. It was also proven that the owner of Monolith Clothing Company had known of the defects but still sold it. It had nearly sunk that company.

Roderick's company, Spirit Gear, offered to pay for the legal fees of the injury victims against Monolith Clothing Company. Although he'd taken precautions to keep his company clear of that battle, he'd had the law firm who represented him represent the injury victims.

Roderick sighed as his mind went back to his problem with Tamara and why she was avoiding him. He couldn't get her out of his mind. But he had to because she was his lawyer and a member of his staff. Roderick needed to keep that in mind and treat as a member of his team. He had more important things to do, like save his company and get ready to push it in the direction he wanted to go. Roderick knew many board members were not going to be happy with the company's new direction. He also knew that those board members were hoping he'd lose this case.

The toxic board members didn't like it when the first court hearing had gone in Roderick's favor. They'd liked it even less when Tamara had made them remove the acting chairman. *God, she was magnificent!* Roderick sighed and fell back in his chair. It was no use. His mind kept coming back to Tamara. He wanted to be close to her and feel her lips on his again. She was so full of passion. Roderick's mind flashed back to the first day he'd seen her on the ski slopes when she'd rammed into him. He knew he'd been in the way, but Roderick had thought he was the only one on the slopes. He had to stop because his leg was aching a bit, and he was starting to get a blinding headache.

Roderick had been so shocked when she'd knocked into him and in so much pain from falling on his injured leg that his first reaction had been one of anger. He'd regretted it instantly, but Tamara had flown into him, sparking something in him. Their second run-in had also been his fault, as he hadn't been looking where he was going. But each time their bodies had bumped, a jolt of electricity had run through him. Roderick had known almost instantly he'd wanted her. But he was laying low and keeping away from women. Roderick had to keep out of the spotlight and away from any relationships that could cause more damage to his already severely tarnished reputation.

Roderick had fully intended to find Tamara when the court case was over, but fate had smiled on him and delivered her as his lawyer. Now he could get to know her in the guise of a professional capacity. Even though the press had a field day once they'd seen Roderick's new lawyer. Roderick had sent one of his security team to make sure the press didn't hound Tamara. He knew she had been getting chased by various women groups about defending the enemy of women. But Tamara had not let those men haters get to her. He smiled, remembering her come back when the press had stopped her on the courtroom steps and asked her if Roderick had tried his date rape tricks on her yet.

If I thought for one minute Mr. Steele was guilty, I, myself, would be on the opposing counsel taking him to task. Rape is a severe crime, but so is slander with malicious intent to defame a person's character. As the media, it is your job to convey the truth, not scandalous news, to ensure your ratings are high. Because that is also slander, you should all be ashamed of yourself for tarnishing a person's reputation before you have all the facts. Our constitution dictates that a person is innocent until proven guilty by a jury of his peers upon being presented with all the evidence. Yet the media condemned Mr. Steele and badly tarnished his reputation without having all the proof of nothing more than a sensational headline. Now that the evidence favors Mr. Steele's innocence, you are looking for more gossip by trying to sensationalize my professional relationship with him.

Tamara had handled the press amazingly. Roderick sighed again. He had to find a way to see her again, not one of her team. He sat and thought for a minute before an idea came to him. Roderick was going to adjust the conditions of their business arrangement. That had been one of his conditions that he got to revise his conditions. Roderick grinned and took out his phone. He dialed Tamara's number, and to his surprise, she picked up.

"Hello, Roderick," Tamara's cool voice sent a warm shiver down his spine even when she was frosty.

"Hello, Tamara," Roderick smiled. "I haven't seen you in a while, only your minions."

"I've been busy, and I'm sure my highly qualified and competent team members would not appreciate being called minions," Tamara advised Roderick.

"I'm sorry I called them minions," Roderick apologized. "They are very sharp ladies that are driven and dedicated."

"Is there something I can do for you, Roderick?" Tamara asked him. "I'm due in a meeting in fifteen minutes, and I still have a lot to prepare for it."

"Will you have dinner with me tomorrow night?" Roderick asked her.

"I don't think so, Roderick," Tamara told him.

"How about I change the condition of our business arrangement," Roderick said. "If you have dinner with me at this secluded little restaurant I know tomorrow night, I'll answer any five questions you have for me."

"You're going to have to answer my questions anyway, Roderick," Tamara reminded him. "It's up to you whether you want to do it on the stand without being prepped. Or before you're called to the stand already prepped."

"Okay, I guess I'll have to come clean to Thomas," Roderick sighed.

"Fine," Tamara sighed. "Tomorrow night. Give me the name of the restaurant."

"Instead of sending you the name, I'll send my driver to fetch you at seven-thirty tomorrow night," Roderick grinned, and his heartbeat quickened at the thought of spending time with her.

"Okay," Tamara breathed. "I'll see you tomorrow night. But Roderick, you're going to have to come into the office so we can prepare you to take the stand."

"Deal," Roderick said before saying goodbye and hung up.

FOURTEEN

Irresistible

TAMARA WAS ENJOYING HERSELF. RODERICK HAD NOT SENT his driver to fetch her. Instead, he'd fetched her himself. The restaurant was in a secluded part of town, and Roderick knew the owner. The meal was superb. When Tamara had noted that Roderick was not drinking alcohol, she'd opted not to have any either. Tamara had noticed that she'd never seen Roderick touch any alcohol when they'd been together. Whenever he'd offered her wine, Roderick would drink club soda or water.

"Why don't you drink alcohol?" Tamara asked Roderick.

"I don't touch the stuff," Roderick shrugged.

"Since when?" Tamara frowned.

"It must've been June last year," Roderick told her.

"That was the same month the sisters came forward with their accusations," Tamara said. "What made you stop drinking?"

"I had an accident," Roderick told her truthfully. "I had also started to have blackouts."

"Blackouts?" Tamara's brows drew together. "How much were you drinking?"

"I can't remember," Roderick swallowed. "After my fiancée left me, I was pretty broken up. Then, I found out a rival company, Monolith Clothing Company was making knock-offs of my product."

"You lost your first tournament at the beginning of last year," Tamara nodded. "May I ask what happened between you and your fiancée?"

"I was engaged to Mila Blake," Roderick watched Tamara's eyebrows rise up.

"The supermodel Mila Blake?" Tamara asked.

"Yes," Roderick nodded. "I was head over heels in love with her. Well, at least I thought I was." He shook his head. "We'd been engaged for almost four years when I found out that she'd been cheating on me for two of those four years."

"I'm sorry," Tamara felt for Roderick.

"That wasn't the worst part," Roderick pinched the bridge of his nose. "It was what almost ripped my family apart."

"Why would it rip your family apart?" Tamara looked confused.

"Mila got married two months after she broke off our engagement," Roderick leaned forward and cupped his soda glass, giving a small laugh. "I was invited to the wedding." He took a sip of the soda. "Not only was I invited, but I was supposed to be one of the groomsmen."

"What?" Tamara couldn't believe what she was hearing. Who'd steal Roderick's fiancée and still want him to be a groomsman?

"Believe me, the groom didn't even want me at the wedding, but he was forced to ask me to be a groomsman," Roderick shook his head, staring into his glass.

"Am I missing something?" Tamara frowned.

"You really don't keep up with celebrities, do you?" Roderick gave her a small smile.

"No," Tamara admitted. "I don't like wading through tabloid trash."

"I think your speech to the press the other day let the whole of California know how you felt about the press and media," Roderick grinned. "So you don't know who Mila Blake's husband is?"

"No, I don't," Tamara admitted, but she was beginning to get a feeling she might.

"His name is Jaylon," Roderick took another sip of his soda, "and he's my older brother."

"Your brother?" Tamara nearly choked on her water. "Jaylon …" She frowned. *Roderick's older brother was his half-brother.* Something niggled at the back of Tamara's mind.

"Yes," Roderick nodded.

Tamara could see the hurt and betrayal flash in Roderick's eyes.

"I take it you and your older brother don't get along?" Tamara gave him a small smile.

"We used," Roderick told her, "but that is another story altogether."

"Roderick, why was Jaylon Vance elected acting chairman of your company?" Tamara frowned. "Why would the board of directors elect the alleged former owner of Monolith Clothing Company?"

"Jaylon Vance is my older brother," Roderick frowned at her. "I thought you knew that?"

"Uh… no," Tamara said wide-eyed.

Why hadn't any of this come up in her research? A chill crept up Tamara's spine thinking she may know what it was that she felt she was missing or overlooking in Roderick's case. While Tamara had been going over

Roderick's case, she couldn't help but feel there was more going on. The case wasn't only about defaming Roderick. It had been a huge shock to find out that Jaylon Vance was Roderick's brother. Roderick hadn't told Tamara any of his family's names. She'd found out about Roderick's family's names through her research, and for some reason, Jaylon had been listed as Jaylon Steele, not Vance.

Jaylon and Roderick hardly bore any resemblance to one another either. Jaylon's father had been a Native American. Jaylon was tall, extremely handsome, with deep brown eyes, chiseled features, and jet black hair. In contrast, Roderick was tall, with dark brown hair and brown eyes. Roderick was more ruggedly handsome. What Tamara was wondering was why she'd never linked Jaylon's wife to her being a supermodel. However, she'd never discussed anything personal with the man, so his wife had never been mentioned.

"That must've felt like an awful betrayal," Tamara shook her head. "Have you and your brother always been so competitive?" She asked Roderick curiously. "I mean, he opened up a rival company. Even his products are basically the same as yours."

"I know, things have been rough between Jaylon and me since I opened Spirit Gear," Roderick pulled a face and took a deep breath. "Jaylon opened his company a year before my engagement ended." He twirled his glass, staring into the liquid. "I wasn't even aware Monolith Clothing Company was owned by Jaylon until one of my engineers pointed out they were making inferior knock-offs of our products.

"Oh no," Tamara breathed. "That must've been such a blow for you."

"The biggest blow was my parents investing in Jaylon's company and backing him," Roderick blew out a breath.

"Your parents!" Tamara couldn't imagine her parents betraying her like that.

"I left it alone until a few of Monolith Clothing Company's products were found to be defective because of the materials they were using," Roderick pinched the bridge of his nose and shook his head. "A few people were injured because of their gear. Because the product was so similar to mine, the customers tried to sue my company." Roderick's hand shook as he took another sip of his soda. "My lawyers managed to prove it was not our product and that it was a Monolith Clothing Company product."

"That must've been a relief for you," Tamara swallowed, and her heart thudded.

"The injured victims have already been through hell. They'd lost their claims against my company," Roderick ran his hand through his hair. "I felt so bad because I knew it was my brother's fault these people were suffering. So I offered to pay my law firm to take the victims on in their fight against Monolith Clothing Company who had known about the defects."

"You were the mysterious benefactor that helped the injured victims," Tamara smiled at him.

"I wouldn't say, benefactor. I was trying to appease some of my own demons," Roderick admitted. "Do you know about that case against Monolith Clothing Company?" He looked at her questioningly.

"Yes," Tamara cleared her throat and looked away from him guiltily. "I was the lawyer representing Jaylon and Monolith Clothing Company." She looked back at him and saw the shock on his face.

"You were the vicious hell-cat?" Roderick frowned. *Why hadn't his research on Tamara brought this up?*

"No," Tamara knew who he was talking about. "I took over the case from Pamela Clay, she was taken ill partway through the trial, and I had to step in. She was known as the Hellcat." she laughed.

"Oh, okay," Roderick nodded. *That made sense.* "My lawyers were having a hard time with that case. Then out of the blue, a lead landed in their lap, and they managed to turn it around."

"That's why I lost!" Tamara looked away as her cheeks colored. She placed her glass on the table, getting her guilty thoughts under control. "But the other side deserved to win that case. That one young girl will be scarred for life and never walk without the help of a cane again."

"I couldn't believe my brother would be so negligent," Roderick breathed. "That was so unlike Jaylon, but I guess circumstances change us all. I'd hit rock bottom and was trying to float my way back up to the top by the time that case was going on."

"Oh, Roderick," Tamara reached out and covered his hand with hers. "You've been through a lot over these last few years."

"I had lost the last skiing competition of the year because I'd hit the rails and started to drown my sorrows in whisky and whoring around," Roderick swallowed. "My second-in-command kept warning me to pull it together and did whatever he could to keep the Spirit Gear going." He shook his head. "Then I had a skiing accident. I was injured and hurt someone close to me who was trying to save me. You see, I went skiing in a drunken stupor."

"What happened?" Tamara looked at Roderick wide-eyed.

"I couldn't tell you as I was having one of my black-outs," Roderick frowned. "All I remembered was feeling like I was dreaming the entire thing. When I woke up in the hospital, it was with that feeling when you come out of a nightmare."

"What did you drink the night before?" Tamara frowned. Something about the way Roderick had described how he was feeling on the ski slope didn't sound right.

"That's the thing," Roderick told her, looking up into her eyes. "I remember going to bed early that night because I was going to practice on the black glacier ski run."

"You don't remember drinking?" Tamara's brows furrowed together tighter.

"No," Roderick shook his head. He was feeling a little embarrassed admitting to Tamara that he had a drinking problem.

"Did someone see you out drinking the night before the accident?" Tamara asked him. "Who was with you on that trip?"

"My younger brother, Sam," Roderick told her. "And no, my brother had gone to bed at the same time I did. Sam had said he was feeling tired. He could hardly keep his eyes open through dinner. I think the altitude of the ski resort was getting to him."

"Your brother, Sam," Tamara bit her bottom lip. "He wasn't involved with Jaylon's company?"

"Hell, no," Roderick shook his head. "Sam would never do that to me. We may have our differences, and he can be a right dick that needs a leash at times, but he would never betray me."

"Was it Sam who got hurt?" Tamara asked.

"Yes," Roderick nodded. "He snapped his leg."

"How awful," Tamara shuddered, watching the guilt flicker in Roderick's eyes.

Tamara started to get a better picture of what may be at the root of Roderick's current predicament as she began to piece more of the puzzle together.

FIFTEEN

A Blossoming Romance

ON THE DRIVE HOME FROM THE RESTAURANT, TAMARA told Roderick about Zach and how she'd ended up at Salt Lake on her skiing trip. She admitted to Roderick that the Monolith Clothing Company case had been the first case Tamara had lost. She told him how that case had started the domino effect losing streak for her, ending her employment at her old firm. There were things about the Monolith Clothing Company case that Tamara had not told anyone, not even Nicole, and she was not ready to share them. But it had put a bad taste in her mouth for defending the clients she'd been defending.

Roderick walked Tamara to her door. Tamara opened her front door and turned to look up at Roderick. Her heart pounded in her chest, and butterflies were going wild in her stomach. She was standing close to him and could smell his cologne and feel his body's warmth.

"Would you like to come up for a coffee," Tamara said softly.

"I would," Roderick's voice was deep and husky. "But only if you're sure."

Tamara smiled and nodded before turning and leading him inside.

"You can put your car keys in the…." Tamara threw her keys in the bowl on her side cabinet inside the door at the same time she did.

Their hands touched, and they both froze as their eyes locked. Tamara wasn't sure who made the first move. Since their first meeting, the sexual tension that sizzled between them drew them together, and she found herself wrapped in Roderick's powerful arms. His lips devoured hers while their hands explored each other's bodies. Soon they were both naked, and Tamara was being lifted so she could wrap her legs around Roderick's waist. He backed her against the wall while his hot lips roamed her needy flesh until she thought she was going to explode with longing to feel him join her.

"Tamara," Roderick rasped as his eyes, dark with desire, met hers. "You're so beautiful." His voice was hoarse as he thrust forward to satiate her need.

Tamara called out and dug her nails into the taunt muscled flesh of his back as she gave herself over to mind-blowing pleasure.

THE NEXT FEW weeks flew by, and Tamara and Roderick spent every spare moment they could together. She and Roderick couldn't seem to get enough of each other. They were careful, though, as they couldn't let their relationship leak out. It would not be professional, and both Roderick and Tamara had reputations they were trying to repair, not tarnish more.

Unfortunately, Nicole had caught Roderick at Tamara's home on more than one occasion. Nicole was not happy about it, but Tamara knew she could count on her best friend to keep quiet about it. On the weekends, Roderick took Tamara out of the city and away from prying eyes. It allowed them to go for long walks on the beach and explore the quiet little towns they went to. They were getting to know each other and were getting to a point where they couldn't bear to spend a night alone. One night, Roderick had landed on her doorstep at one in the morning, claiming he couldn't sleep without her by his side.

Tamara felt like she was walking on cloud nine. On Friday, they were going away for the weekend, so Tamara took the day off to do some shopping for the trip. While she was at the shopping mall, she ran into Zach. He told Tamara that he was back with Stella and they were engaged. Tamara congratulated him and told him she'd been dating again as well but kept *the who* she'd been dating to herself. The court case would be over soon, and then she could tell the world she was dating Roderick Miles. Until then, it was hers and Roderick's secret.

Tamara met Roderick at their designated meeting spot, and she was surprised to see him in the town car with his chauffeur.

"Hi," Tamara slid into the car once the driver had put her purchases in the trunk.

"Hi, yourself," Roderick smiled at her, stealing a quick kiss. "You look ravishing in that sexy sundress." His voice was hoarse as his eyes ran over her long tanned legs.

The car pulled off but didn't head in the direction Tamara expected. Instead, it was heading in the direction of Roderick's house.

"Where are we going?" Tamara asked Roderick with a frown.

"A change of plans, I'm afraid," Roderick told her. "I

have some urgent business to attend to tomorrow, so I thought we could go back to my place and have a nice romantic evening."

"Sounds good," Tamara smiled at him.

On the drive back to Roderick's house, his phone rang. Tamara's hair prickled at the back of her neck when she heard him say he couldn't speak now and would call back later. Tamara refrained from asking who that was. Roderick's mood changed after he hung up the phone. He stared broodily out of the window for the rest of the drive.

—•✣✣•✣✣•—

THAT NIGHT RODERICK wasn't himself. He was edgy, and even when they made love, she could feel he wasn't really with her, and it felt like he was going through the motions. Tamara tried not to let her doubts cloud her mind. She knew the kind of pressure Roderick was under the closer the final court day drew nearer. But Tamara couldn't keep her suspicions at bay. When she woke up in the early hours of the morning to find Roderick was not next to her.

Tamara got up and padded softly through the massive house until she heard his soft voice coming from his study.

"I told you, I'd sort it out when I get there," Roderick said to whoever was on the other end of the line. "This has got to stop. I told you it was over. Fine, how much do you want this time?"

Tamara's brows drew together, and her heart thudded against her rib cage. *Who was Roderick talking to?*

"Jesus," Roderick breathed. "But if it'll shut you up and stop these midnight calls, I'll deposit it into your account in a little while." He went quiet. "Yes. It'll hit your account right away. Stop panicking. No one knows I promise you. I love you too." She heard Roderick sigh.

Tamara's whole body felt numb and frozen with shock. *I love you too?* She heard Roderick moving and quickly ran back to the bedroom and dove beneath the sheets. Tamara lay awake torturously, waiting for Roderick to come back to bed. She'd started to doze off almost two hours later when she felt the bed dip, and Roderick slid carefully beneath the covers. Her heart was beating so loudly Tamara was sure Roderick could hear it. She waited for him to turn and snuggle into her, but he didn't. Instead, he kept to his side of the bed.

SIXTEEN

Rivalry

TAMARA DIDN'T KNOW HOW SHE'D MANAGED TO FALL asleep after Roderick had come back to bed, but she had, and when she woke up the next morning, Roderick was gone. He'd left a note for her on his pillow.

HI, Sleeping Beauty. Sorry I had to catch an early flight for business. Make yourself some breakfast. The staff has the day off, but my driver is there when you're ready to go. I'll be back in a few days and well before the court date to prepare for the trial. I miss you already and can't wait to get back to you.

   Roderick

TAMARA FELT LET down and hurt. Roderick had not said anything to her about going away on business. Tamara wanted to know who he was talking to the previous night in the car and later in his study.

Tamara's phone bleeped and she looked at it in shock. Was that the time? She'd slept most of the morning away, and it was almost noon. She looked at her messages, and there were a few encrypted messages from her private detective. Tamara had to leave in a hurry. She jumped into Roderick's shower and pulled on one of her new sundresses she'd bought the day before for their canceled weekend trip. Tamara's heart felt heavy as Roderick's driver took her to a cafe. Tamara didn't have time to dwell on what was or wasn't going on between her and Roderick. She had a case to win, and then she could decide what she would do about Roderick. When the driver dropped her off, she waited until he was out of sight before ordering an Uber.

Callum, her PI, was being secretive. Whatever he had for Tamara must be highly sensitive for him to be scared. Callum was ex-military black ops, and Tamara trusted him. She'd given him a chance when no one else would. He'd been injured on an assignment. It had lost him an eye, and he had a jagged scar down the side of his face. But he was still a very sexy man in a dangerous sort of way. Tamara had helped Callum get set up as a private detective and get his license to work for law firms. He was loyal to Tamara and would drop anything to help her. So when Callum was this secretive, Tamara knew something was not right with Roderick's case. Just like she'd suspected all along.

"CALLUM, are you sure this information is correct?" Tamara looked at Callum in shock.

"It is," Callum assured her. "Take note of the dates the

company, Arcane Gear first opened." He pointed to the paper.

"That was almost a year before Roderick's company, Spirit Gear, opened," Tamara frowned. "I need to know some more information about who runs or owns Arcane Gear." She shook her head. "Their products are almost exactly the same as both Roderick's and Jaylon's."

"Arcane Gear nearly closed its doors when Roderick's company started up and took over the market," Callum explained to Tamara. "Arcane Gear was barely making ends meet, and the company was forced to close its doors when the chairman committed suicide."

Tamara frowned at the timeline of events. Something niggled at her, and she had a feeling there was a bigger picture to be seen. And Arcane Gear was somehow involved. It seemed like Arcane Gear had gone from shutting its doors to a multimillion-dollar company overnight. Now Arcane Gear was trying to acquire both Roderick's and Jaylon's company. Something about the new company's name had alarm bells ringing in Tamara's head until it dawned on her where she'd heard it before.

"Callum, I need to know everything you can get me on Arcane Gear," Tamara told him. "I want to know who owns it, who injected the cash into it, who started it, and everything else you can dig up."

"On it," Callum assured her. "Oh, and Tamara," His eyes looked at her warningly. "Watch you back. Arcane Gear has been linked with some pretty dirty deeds. It seems whoever gets in their way is 'taken care of' if you know what I mean."

Tamara shuddered. "Thanks for the warning." That icy feeling ran up her spine again.

"Don't leave with those folders," Callum told her. "I'll get them to your house."

"Thank you, Callum." Tamara shuddered again. She also felt there was a lot Callum was keeping from her, but also knew he'd only do that if he thought he was protecting her. "I have to go see Nicole. I think I know where I've heard of Arcane Gear before."

"Be careful," Callum warned her.

"Oh and there's one more thing I need you to do for me," Tamara told him.

Tamara wrote a number on a piece of paper and gave Callum instructions for what she needed him to do. She had a slight twinge of conscience when she did, but she hardened her heart. It needed to be done!

—•᷂᷂᷀᷀·᷂᷂᷀᷀•—

"I'LL GET the information for you," Nicole assured Tamara. "I would've thought now that you're so involved with the Steele family you could ask them yourself." She said with a hint of sarcasm in her voice.

They were having a small late lunch at their favorite cafe.

"I know you're only trying to look out for me in your own weird way," Tamara told her friend. "So I'm going to let that slide."

"Tamara, you could've been happily engaged to Zach," Nicole reasoned with Tamara. "You know he's still in love with you. I'm sorry, but he is still one of Elias's friends."

"I know you are in the middle of this Zach and my thing," Tamara sighed. "But, Nicole, I was over Zach long before the ski trip to Salt Lake was over."

"You didn't seem over him," Nicole said.

"I was down because I have a mortgage, bills, and a financial portfolio," Tamara told Nicole. "I needed a job to keep my head above water and protect what I'd built on my own without my parents' help."

"I've always admired that about you," Nicole smiled. "Your father was the freakin' Chief Justice of California and your mother a top surgeon. You didn't need to fight to open doors, you could've had your father or mother pave your way, but you didn't.'."

"You know how I feel about people not working for what they want or blaming others for their hardships," Tamara smiled at Nicole. "I would've been a total hypocrite if I'd let my father make my life easy for me."

"I think the only time you ever used your father's position was for me," Nicole said softly. "When you petitioned for your father to get custody of me when my parents died." Her eyes still filled with tears when she thought of her parents.

"Oh, Merry," Tamara handed her a napkin to wipe her tears. "My parents had already set those wheels in motion. Your parents were my parents' dearest friends. There was no way they'd let you go into a state home or foster care."

"It wasn't only that," Nicole smiled. "You worked your way through college when you could've just relied on your trust fund."

"You worked through college as well," Tamara reminded Nicole. "I seem to remember

You also have quite a tidy trust fund."

"Can you never let someone compliment you?" Nicole sighed. "No, it's embarrassing, and I never worked as hard as I did to get a compliment," Tamara told Nicole. "I did it for the sense of achievement and to know everything I have worked for," she said proudly. "Now, can we change the subject, please?"

"Sure," Nicole took a sip of her wine. "How about you

tell me about your entanglement with a billionaire playboy who's been accused of raping not one but numerous women."

"Nicole!" Tamara hissed. "No, I'm not discussing this with you, and since when did you judge someone before they were proven guilty? You're a lawyer, for God's sake."

"I don't want you getting hurt or being entangled in whatever scandal is going to follow his trial," Nicole told Tamara honestly.

SEVENTEEN

Was Roderick Framed?

TAMARA WAS FEELING HURT AND ANGRY. RODERICK WAS not coming back as scheduled, which meant they didn't have as much time to get him ready to take the stand as they needed to. It also meant Tamara had to wait another week to see him and find out what the hell was going on with him, or rather their relationship. Tamara was tired of getting an earful of warnings from Nicole and her smug *I told you so* looks about Tamara's relationship with Roderick.

Tamara felt like she was getting an ulcer, trying to keep Nicole off her back and worrying about her relationship with Roderick. Tamara still had to find out who Roderick was on the phone to the night before he left town. All she knew was that he'd deposited a large sum of money into an off-shore account, and Callum was still trying to find out whose account it was.

What was getting to Tamara was that Roderick wasn't picking up any of her calls or answering any of her texts. Roderick wasn't even taking any calls from her office. As a result, the investigation into his case has slowed to a halt. The sisters had become uncooperative and were refusing to talk to her. Their brother had not been happy when he'd found out who Tamara was and had tried to claim she'd coerced information from him. Only Tamara had recorded their entire conversation at the bar, and he didn't have a leg to stand on.

Tamara had warned the man on numerous occasions during the night he should not be speaking to anyone about an ongoing case. He'd said he didn't care if she was the FBI. He'd still say what he wanted to say. The sisters' lawyer had tried to make Roderick settle with the sisters and make a statement in the press admitting to his crimes. But of course, that wasn't happening on Tamara's watch. She now knew that Roderick might have been framed, and with all the evidence she'd gathered, she was sure she could prove. All she needed was for her client to be back in LA!

Three nights before Roderick was to appear in court, he still wasn't back in Los Angeles. Tamara was in a huff when she let herself into her apartment. She nearly died of fright when she found the curtain in her living room closed, and Callum was sitting in there. He was not alone.

"Callum, what the hell?" Alicia hissed, turning on the light and freezing when a familiar face stared back at her.

Anger and hurt churned inside Tamara as her eyes narrowed. "Where the hell have you been, Roderick?" Her voice was frosty.

"Tamara, is it?" Roderick frowned at her. "Oh, now I know where I've seen you before."

Tamara frowned and stepped back away from Roderick. There was something different about him. Roderick looked at her as if he didn't know her at all. Tamara felt tears burning at the back of her eyes. A shiver of familiarity crept up her spine. Roderick's eyes slowly traveled over her body before he looked up at her with a grin on his face.

"What kind of game are you playing?" Tamara looked at her wide-eyed. Was he schizophrenic, maybe?

"Tamara," Callum stood up next to her. "This is Sam Steele, Roderick Miles's identical twin brother."

"That was you on the airplane?" Tamara hissed as she glared at Sam Steele. He was an identical copy of Roderick right down to the smirk on his face.

"Oh, you thought it was Roderick?" Sam laughed. "I bet he loved that!"

"Sam," Callum warned him. "If you disrespect Tamara, our deal is off."

"Deal?" Tamara frowned at Callum. "What is going on, Callum." She ignored Sam.

"I found Callum sniffing around the company I'm working at," Sam told Tamara.

"You work for Roderick's rival company?" Tamara looked at him, amazed.

"No," Sam shook his head. "I'm doing research, let's say."

"Sam is Roderick's investigator and right-hand man," Callum explained to Tamara. "It was Sam who made sure the research I gave you the other day fell into your hands."

"In return, Callum has agreed to team up and work with me," Sam told Alicia. "He gets medical, the hours are bad, but the pay is excellent."

So Sam is the joker of the family, Alicia thought.

"Sam's company does a lot of good," Callum explained to Tamara. "But I will fill you in on that later. Sam is here because he hasn't been able to get hold of Roderick since he left LA."

"I haven't been able to get hold of him either," Tamara's brows knitted together once again.

"I think Roderick may be in danger," Sam became serious, making Tamara shudder. Now she saw the dangerous side of Sam Steele. She knew, like Callum, that was not the side you ever wanted to be. "You need to see something."

Callum handed Tamara a file. She opened it and started to read it. Her eyes were huge when she'd finished scanning the contents.

"I was in the army when Roderick started his first company," Sam told Tamara. "Roderick and Jaylon started the first Arcane Gear, together with one of Roderick's ski buddies, Keegan, who was also one of his best friends."

"Jaylon was Roderick's and Keegan's skiing manager and coach," Callum continued the story. "Jaylon was married before he married Mila. His first wife was expecting their first baby when there was a horrible car accident, and his wife was killed on impact."

"How tragic," Tamara breathed.

"About a week before Jaylon's wife's accident, was when the blow-up between Roderick and Keegan happened," Sam told Tamara. "To this day, no one knows what the blow-up was about."

"Whatever it was, it was enough for Roderick to walk out," Callum said. "Jaylon was trying to mend the rift between the two men, but neither of them would tell him what it was about."

"A week later, Roderick was driving Jaylon's wife some-where, "Sam frowned. "We're still not clear on where or why they were in the car together. Roderick lost control of the car, and Jaylon's wife was killed. Roderick didn't have a scratch on him."

"Why do you look like something doesn't add up to you?" Tamara asked Sam.

"I was on leave from the army, and I saw that car," Sam shook his head. "There was no way Roderick walked away from that accident without a scratch."

"Here," Callum handed Tamara the photo of the car. "See for yourself, and this is Roderick right after the accident."

"Jesus," Tamara breathed. "So, what are you saying?"

"Roderick would never speak about the accident," Sam told Tamara. "The cops ruled it an accident and Roderick was let off. A few days after the accident, Keegan took his own life." He ran his hand through his hair. "Jaylon and Roderick had a huge falling out. Jaylon couldn't forgive Roderick for killing his wife."

"Jaylon felt even more betrayed when he learned that Roderick had started a new company, Spirit Gear. Roderick had started it five months before walking out of Arcane Gear," Callum continued.

"Shit," Tamara had a bad feeling.

"When Keegan killed himself, Jaylon couldn't sustain the Arcane Gear, especially when Roderick had taken all his patents with him," Sam breathed. "Jaylon had no option but to shut Arcane Gear's doors."

"Was it Jaylon who breathed life back into Arcane Gear?" Tamara couldn't understand why Jaylon would do that.

"No," Sam shook his head. "That's what I was doing at Arcane Gear: trying to figure out who bought the company from Jaylon. I was also trying to figure out where they got the kind of capital injection they needed to get it to where it currently is in the marketplace."

"Whoever it is, they're trying to bring down both Jaylon's and Roderick's company," Tamara walked over to her briefcase and took out a folder Nicole had given her. "Arcane Gear was the company that sold Monolith Clothing Company inferior products to make their skis with."

"I thought that was a smaller company that Jaylon sued

and closed down," Sam took the other report Tamara handed him.

"That smaller company was part of Arcane Gear," Tamara told Callum and Sam.

"Why didn't this evidence come to light in Jaylon's court case?" Sam asked.

"It was a file that went missing from my records," Tamara told Sam. "I asked Nicole to look for it at my old firm again. But she couldn't find it, but my paralegal's boyfriend did." She shook her head. "That file was what would've helped Jaylon's case. He was still guilty of knowing the skiing equipment was defective, though."

"What is your paralegal's boyfriend, some kind of hacker?" Sam asked.

"Moving on," Tamara avoided the topic of Georgia's boyfriend. "You think that whoever's after Roderick is after more than his company?"

"You're as bright as Callum and Roderick say you are," Sam smiled.

Tamara could see the difference between Roderick and Sam the more she spoke to Sam.

Roderick was in danger, and she was about to inform the police when Sam and Callum told her not to handle it. Tamara needed to keep the information they'd given her to herself. So instead, they gave her the evidence and information she needed to win Roderick's case for him.

EIGHTEEN

Evidence

IT WAS SATURDAY, AND MONDAY WAS RODERICK'S CASE. Tamara had not heard a word from him since he'd left LA. Callum and Sam had also gone dark on her, and she was left with a bag full of information she could do nothing with. Tamara knew she was pushing herself, but running was the only way to calm the anger and tension coiling inside of her.

As she ran back to her house, a delivery van pulled up with a package for her. She signed for it with a frown on her face when it was marked as confidential evidence for her. Tamara looked at the box as she walked into her living room. She had a bottle of water and opened the package. Alicia felt shock waves tingle down her spine as she went through it.

Tamara knew what the blow-up between Keegan and Roderick was about. Roderick had been using Arcane Gear funds to start Spirit Gear. The patents Roderick claimed were his belonged to Keegan. Roderick hadn't left Arcane Gear. Keegan had kicked him out. But Steele Gear was already starting to boom in the marketplace because Roderick Miles's name was linked to it.

The more alarming evidence against Roderick was that he'd only got his first Olympic gold medal because Keegan, who apparently was the better skier, had broken his arm. Keegan had been pushed down a flight of stairs the night before the competition and couldn't compete. Although it was never proven, a witness was sure they'd seen Roderick Miles push Keegan down the stairs after an argument.

The evidence that stole Tamara's breath away was the reason why Roderick was in the car with Jaylon's wife. Roderick and Jaylon's wife had been having an affair, and the baby she was carrying was Roderick's, not Jaylon's. The day they were in the car together was when Roderick had found out for definite the baby was his. Once again, it could never be proven, but it was suspected that Roderick had deliberately crashed the car to get rid of Jaylon's wife and the problems she would cause him.

Tamara stood staring at the documents feeling sick and cold. Keegan had taken his own life because he was heavily in debt, and Roderick was trying to buy Keegan's silence. He couldn't take the burden as all the company debt fell on his shoulders. Somewhere deep in her mind, Tamara knew she should question everything she'd read in the box. Hell, she should be asking where the evidence had come from. Some part of her knew nothing added or made sense. But the hurt and angry part of her smarting over being rejected by Roderick clung to the evidence as the truth. If Roderick was capable of what she'd read, he was most certainly capable of rape.

Tamara was in shock as she realized that Roderick Miles cared about no one else but Roderick Miles. No wonder his fiancée had left him for Jaylon, who'd, tried to help Roderick. He'd even wanted to amalgamate Spirit Gear with Monolith Clothing Company. Still, Roderick had laughed him off, according to the information she'd just received. Jaylon and Roderick's parents had needed Roderick's help, and he'd turned their backs on. After everything Roderick had already put Jaylon through, Roderick had turned his back on his family. He had his fame and fortune but had got it all through deception.

Tamara's heart screamed at her to be reasonable and fact check before she condemned Roderick. But her mind was made up. She would win this case for Roderick, and with the evidence she had, she would rip the sister's case to shreds. Roderick was once again going to walk away squeaky clean. His reputation will be restored so he could cheat himself to another gold medal and get his precious company back. Tamara wished she could walk away now and not have to see Roderick Miles ever again. But she couldn't quit now. She needed a win to restore her reputation, which made her no better than Roderick.

Nicole was going to have a field day with this, so Tamara decided not to tell her best friend about it. Tamara couldn't discuss the case anyway. She called Callum to say she had a box full of evidence that arrived on her doorstep and asked him if he'd sent it to her.

"No," Callum told her on the phone. "I don't think Sam sent you anything either."

"I doubt this evidence came from Sam," Tamara told him. "It's pretty damning stuff for Roderick Miles."

"Do you want me to fetch it and verify it?" Callum asked her.

"You can fetch it," Tamara shrugged. "I don't want this stuff in my house."

"Okay, leave in the living room. I'll pop past later when you're not at home to get it," Callum told her.

"Thank you, Callum," Tamara sighed, feeling down. "Any luck tracking down Roderick?"

"Yes," Callum told her, "I think we've found him. I have to go. I'll check in with you before the court on Monday."

After Tamara hung up from Callum, she met with Nicole and hoped that the box of damning evidence would be gone when she got home.

NINETEEN

It's Time to Quit!

TAMARA WALKED INTO COURT, SURPRISED TO SEE RODERICK already there and seated with Georgia, Tamara's paralegal. She'd asked Georgia to place herself in the middle between her and Roderick. When Georgia had looked at Tamara's request questioningly, she'd said that the media were already having a field day with her being Roderick's lawyer. Georgia was recently engaged, so the dynamics would look better with Georgia sitting in between them.

Georgia had seemed to accept Tamara's explanation, thank goodness. She couldn't tell her paralegal that she was revolted by the mere thought of sitting near Roderick. A tiny voice in the back of her head said to her that was not true, but Tamara ignored it. Instead, she kept the ice around her heart and walked into the courtroom. Tamara was surprised to see Sam there, who greeted her with a cheeky grin. She shook her head at him and headed to her seat.

"Hello, Tamara," Roderick leaned over and gave her a warm smile.

"Hello, Roderick," Tamara said frostily. "I hope you

found some time to go over the notes and advise Georgia put together for you?"

"I didn't," Roderick surprised her by saying. "I want to apologize for not being able to get back when I said I would." He couldn't finish what he was saying because the judge arrived and the court was in session.

Roderick surprised Tamara and did surprisingly well up on the stand. One look at the jury, and she knew Roderick had managed to pull the wool over their eyes and won their hearts. Tamara had to physically stop herself from rolling her eyes throughout his testimony. She proved to the jury that Roderick did not drug nor have his way with the woman, nor did he pay anyone off to keep quiet about his alleged perversion. Roderick's skiing accident had shown he was the one who'd been drugged. Tamara also showed that the videos of him were faked.

Tamara also proved that Roderick was being discredited so another company, Arcane Gear, could maneuver Roderick's company, Spirit Gear, into a position where the company would be an easy takeover target. Arcane Gear would be set to become one of the biggest sportswear companies in the marketplace. The sister's brother was, in fact, a disgruntled employee of Spirit Gear and had been paid to help Arcane Gear get Roderick disgraced.

The court ruled in favor of Roderick, and all charges against him were dropped.

"Congratulations, Roderick," Tamara nodded coolly, "If you'll excuse us, we have to get back to the office to file the reports. I'm sure you'll want to go celebrate with your family."

Before Roderick had time to react or say anything, Tamara ushered Georgia out of the courtroom.

"I'M SO glad you could make dinner," Tamara clinked her wine glass to Nicole's.

"I'm glad to be here. Your parents are my parents too." Nicole grinned. "I've missed them since they've been retired and traveling the world." She shook her head. "I get a little envious when I get sent all their pictures."

"Well, my mom is going to be upset that you didn't bring Aiden," Tamara referred to Nicole's five-year-old son. "She's been missing him."

"I know," Nicole sighed. "But Elias and I hardly get any time to ourselves."

"I'm having dinner at my house tomorrow night," Tamara told her. "I'm cooking."

"Oh," Nicole's eyes narrowed. "You've broken it off with the billionaire, haven't you?"

"I don't want to talk about it," Tamara gave Nicole a small smile. "I do want to apologize for my behavior, though. I've not been very nice to you these last months."

"No, you haven't," Nicole agreed, "and it's going to cost you a spa day to make up for it."

"Deal, but it's going to have to wait for a while," Tamara grinned at the frown on Nicole's face. "What are you up to?"

"There are my darling girls and Elias," Tamara's mother grinned as she and Tamara's father rushed into the restaurant. "Where's my grandson?" She looked accusingly at Elias and Nicole.

"You can see him tomorrow night at Tamara's for dinner," Nicole grinned and transferred the limelight to Tamara.

"Oh," Mrs. Decker sat in between Nicole and Tamara. "Well done on your big win, Tamara."

"You must be proud," Mr. Decker beamed at Tamara. "Are you enjoying being at the new firm?"

"That is what I wanted to talk to all of you about," Tamara grinned. "I quit today."

All the faces around the table stared at her in shock.

"I'm tired of defending people I don't want to defend," Tamara told her family. "I've decided to start my own small firm. Georgia and Sienna are going to be my first official employees. I'm finally going to put my inheritance and investments to work."

"Honey, that's amazing," Tamara's mother surprised her by saying.

"It's a huge risk, honey," Tamara's father said. "Would you let me help you? I don't practice law anymore, but I can advise."

"What about retirement, dad?" Tamara frowned at her father.

"Your father and I have been traveling for over a year now," Mrs. Decker said. "We want to come back home for a while and be with you girls, our grandson, and son-in-law." She grinned at Elias.

"Does this mean I have a babysitter on hand?" Nicole grinned at Mrs. Decker.

"Honey, anytime you want to leave little Aiden with us, we're there for you," Mrs. Decker smiled.

—•◦⊙•⊙◦•—

TAMARA HAD JUST GOT BACK from the restaurant when her phone rang. She frowned when she saw it was Sam's number. What did Sam want?

"Tamara, don't hang up," Roderick's voice came through the phone. "I need to talk to you."

"I don't think so, Roderick," Tamara said frostily. "I know everything, and I really don't think you and I are going to work out."

"Look, I'll come by your office tomorrow, and I can explain everything," Roderick pleaded.

"No, I don't think so," Tamara told him. "I've quit that job, and I'm no longer your lawyer. I don't want anything to do with you, Roderick. I have to go." She hung up and ignored the myriad of text messages he sent after that.

Tamara felt like her heart was shattered into a million pieces. She got into the shower and had a good cry before falling into bed and having a restless night's sleep.

TWENTY

Bobsledding With Roderick Miles

TAMARA STOPPED BY HER OFFICE TO COLLECT THE LAST OF her personal items and drop off files from Roderick's case. Thomas was sad to see her go but was proud she was branching out on her own and asked her if she needed another attorney who could invest in her firm. She promised to meet up with Thomas to discuss it.

Tamara stopped at the grocery store to stock up on food to cook for dinner on the way home. It had been a long time since she'd cooked a meal at home. As Tamara climbed out of the Uber in front of her house, she breathed in the beginning of her new life. She would finally be her own boss and run her firm the way she and her two employees wanted.

Excitement zinged through her. Tamara knew that her mom, dad, Nicole, Elias, and Aiden were already at her house and let themselves in. Nicole and her mother both had spare keys. Tamara's mom had brought the wine, and Nicole had got dessert. She was looking forward to cooking and being surrounded by her family.

"I'm home," Alicia called, letting herself in. "Can someone please come and help me with the groceries."

"I'm here," Elias popped out of the living room. "What are you going to do, feed an army?" He eyed out all her grocery bags.

"I figured I needed to stock up now that I'd be spending more time at home." Tamara grinned at Elias.

"You have a visitor," Elias whispered. "I'll take care of these, but you'd better get in there before your mother brings out the baby pictures."

"Please tell me it's not Zach," Tamara's face dropped.

"Nope," Elias pulled a face and disappeared laden with bags before Tamara could get any more information from him.

What now! Tamara sighed and walked into the living room. She froze at the door when Roderick lifted his head and smiled at her. Aiden was sitting on Roderick's lap laughing while Tamara's mother, father, and Nicole had been deep in conversation with him.

"What are you doing here, Roderick?" Tamara eyed him out.

"Honey, that's no way to greet your guest," Mrs. Decker stood up and pulled Nicole and her husband with her. "Come on, you two," she bent down and picked up Aiden, "you too, little man. Let's give these two some privacy."

"Apparently, we're going to start the supper you were supposed to cook," Nicole pulled a face at Tamara as Mrs. Decker herded them out of the sitting room.

"Tamara, please hear me out," Roderick jumped right in before Tamara could say anything. "If you don't like what I have to say, I'll leave and never come back again."

"You have ten minutes," Tamara looked at her watch.

"Fair enough," Roderick indicated for her to sit down.

Tamara perched herself on the edge of her chair.

"I know the documents you saw were pretty damning," Roderick started. "My brother showed me. He also told me about the airplane. I was wondering about that, and I apologize for my callus brother."

"He already apologized," Tamara assured Roderick. "You could've told me you had an identical twin brother."

"I thought you already knew," Roderick said. "I never pushed Keegan down the stairs, and he was never the better skier. Keegan slipped, and I was trying to grab him. He suffered from chronic depression and anxiety. He'd get so anxious before a skiing tournament he'd throw up for hours the night before."

"Anyone can say that," Tamara told him.

"My brother Jaylon and my mother were there that night," Roderick told her. "They saw what happened."

"Okay," Tamara shrugged.

"I won all my medals fair and square," Roderick told her. "I pulled out of Arcane Gear because I found Keegan embezzling money to pay off his gambling debts. He was driving the company into the ground. You have no idea how many times I heard him say he was going to stop gambling."

"Did Jaylon know?" Tamara frowned.

"No," Roderick shook his head. "Keegan was a good guy. He had a younger sister that he was putting through college, and his mother was very sick. So he started gambling as a way to turn over a quick buck to pay his debts which were mainly school and medical bills."

"Why didn't he go to you for help," Tamara asked.

"Keegan was from an exceedingly wealthy family that lost all its money when his father got hooked on gambling," Roderick told her. "Keegan was ashamed of how easily he became addicted to the past." He sighed.

"He also didn't want his mother and sister to get stressed out."

"I never met Keegan's sister, went to some fancy boarding school and then a college overseas," Roderick said. "I tried to help him but found I was getting pulled under and that the loan sharks were coming at me. I wanted to get myself and Jaylon out of that environment." He breathed. "I tried so hard to help Keegan, Tamara. I even destroyed my relationship with my family for him."

"How?" Tamara frowned.

"I found out Keegan and Lydia, Jaylon's wife, was having an affair," Roderick ran his hand through his hair. "That's when I left the company. Lydia and Keegan refused to stop seeing each other. They were going to tell Jaylon."

"The baby was Keegan's?" Tamara looked shocked.

"I believe so," Roderick nodded. "The day I was going to meet Jaylon and bring him on board with Spirit Gear was the day Keegan and Lydia confirmed the baby was Keegan's."

"Keegan was driving the car," Tamara put the pieces together. "That's why you weren't hurt."

"Yes," Roderick nodded. "Keegan had been drinking on top of his depression pills. He'd lost control of the vehicle because he was getting drowsy." He swallowed. "I took the fall for Keegan, and after that, everything between myself and my family went south." He gave a sad smile. "The only one to stick by me was Sam."

"Mila was Keegan's sister and the one that was trying to destroy you and Jaylon," Tamara's eyes widened.

"Correct," Roderick sighed. "She knew how things already were between Jaylon and me. She thought I was the one with the gambling and depression problem because that's what Keegan told her."

"So Mila set out to destroy both you and Jaylon because she blamed you both for Keegan's death," Tamara frowned. "Why Jaylon, though?"

"Mila knew about the affair," Roderick looked at Tamara. "Jaylon and my family know the truth now, and we're rebuilding bridges. Would you forgive me and give me a second chance?"

Tamara swallowed as she looked at Roderick.

"I love you, Tamara, and if you let me, I want to spend the rest of my life loving you," Roderick stood and walked towards her.

"I love you too, Roderick," Tamara let Roderick pull her into his arms as his lips met hers. "Does this mean I get to go Bobsledding with Roderick Miles after all?"

"So you did receive my email invitation to come to Salt Lake with me for a holiday?" He grinned and captured her mouth with his.

"I did, and yes, I would love for you to show me the world," Tamara pulled his mouth back down to hers, ignoring the cheers coming from her family.

About the Author

Rose M. Cooper read her first novel when she was eight years old. Since then, she has read tens of novels and twice as many short stories. She, however, did not discover her special knack for writing romance fiction until a decade later.

Now a full-time author with a specialty in contemporary romance, Cooper writes sensual yet relatable love stories designed to hook her readers at first glance. She views writing as another outlet to creativity, and thus has no intentions of setting down her pen just yet. There are many intriguing love stories to be told, and Cooper is set to tell them all.

She hails from New York and currently makes her home in Copiague, New York with her husband, her black cat and her Maine Coon cat. When she is not writing, you will most certainly find her around computers or getting her nose stuck in a book.

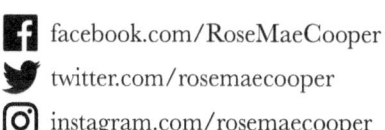

facebook.com/RoseMaeCooper

twitter.com/rosemaecooper

instagram.com/rosemaecooper

Sign Up For My Newsletter To Receive New Release Updates & Specials!

rosemaecooper.com/newsletter

THANKS FOR READING THIS BOOK. PLEASE CONSIDER LEAVING A REVIEW WITH YOUR RETAILER!

www.ingramcontent.com/pod-product-compliance
Lightning Source LLC
Chambersburg PA
CBHW020246150626
46552CB00020B/610